CONQUER

A TALE OF THE NIKA REBELLION IN BYZANTIUM

CONQUER

A TALE OF THE NIKA REBELLION IN BYZANTIUM

BY

JOHN MASEFIELD

NEW YORK

THE MACMILLAN COMPANY

1941

PRINTED IN THE UNITED STATES OF AMERICA
AMERICAN BOOK—STRATFORD PRESS, INC., NEW YORK

NOTE

This story is an account of the very famous Faction struggle which nearly caused the complete destruction of Byzantium in the first week of the year 532.

The tale makes no reference whatever to any living person or existing institution. When it refers to the Dinner-Green and Sea-Blue Factions it alludes to Byzantine parties long since happily extinct, and to no existing parties wearing those or any other colours.

The book is fiction, based on the histories of the sixth century.

CONQUER

A TALE OF THE NIKA REBELLION IN BYZANTIUM

THERE IS NO CITY ON EARTH to be compared with Byzantium, whether for beauty or power: she is the Queen of Cities. When I look down upon her from my window, and see her throned upon her hills, above her port, in the glory of her strangeness, I give thanks to God, that my hand and soul are in the service of so much beauty, directed by so much wisdom.

As there was never before such a City, so, never before were there such rulers as the Emperor, my Master, Justinian, and his most exquisite Consort, our Sovereign Lady the Empress Theodora. They made The City. What I see from my high window and give God thanks for is Their Thought made manifest.

Ignorance among the learned and superstition among the religious may attach importance to other cities. To one who looks out upon this Thought of my Rulers, their claims are as the wind in the leaves, for here, and here only for many centuries, the thought of Rulers has been one with the Thought of God.

Yet I have seen those Rulers almost destroyed by their subjects, and this City, now so magnificent,

brought to ashes from its former strength. For almost a week those subjects did their will till The
City was in ruin. As the body of a man brought
down by fever lies nearly dead, with a raging and
clouded mind, so was this City brought down and
her Ruler daunted by the madnesses of Faction.

Let me try to tell the causes and the course of
this rebellion.

Faction had run (and sometimes raged) in Byzantium for many years. It began, so it is said, in
the differences of mind and view between the feudal, who owned the land and controlled the corn-
markets, and the adventurous, who plied the seas
and brought us the wealth of the world; the one
party is known (usually now contemptuously) as
the Dinner-Greens, with whom the Sea-Blues admit no truce.

The last Emperor but one was a Dinner-Green,
odious for tyranny as for heresy. He was succeeded
by a Sea-Blue, the Uncle of our present Benefactor.
As he grew old, in pain from a neglected wound,
many plots were set against him by the enemies of
his colour. These were brought to naught, now by
daring, now by open battle, so that when this old
Emperor, Justinus, died, the Empire accepted his
nephew Justinian as a successor.

Nearly always, a Nation will give to a young
Ruler first entering upon his task a certain leave
or licence to shew his mettle; people will watch

him, with tolerance and hope, they will support him and forgive his failings, for a time, in the expectation, that in the beginner the first attempts may be followed by the blessings for which men long.

For a time, the people of Byzantium forbore to trouble our young Ruler with comment or riot; they hoped for peace. For some years the reign was quiet; that is outwardly; there were at work within the structure, several forces which later were to join to wreck it.

Chief among these undoubtedly was the enormous force of the Faction of the Dinner-Greens, based on the ownership of vast estates in The City and in the west and upon centuries of privilege and monopoly. The families which owned City property and the land had for centuries held the offices of State and had dispensed all place to their relatives and supporters. They had controlled the Church, the Senate, the Bench, the Provinces and the Army; the ambassadors to foreign Courts were their younger sons while their first-born at home plundered the Treasury. For many years, they had thwarted, while they could, the adventurous trading spirit which used the seas; they had shrunk from the sea, as a rough service not used by gentlemen, and had opposed the growth of a Navy, which had however come into being. In the fifty years before the Rebellion, they had made efforts to null the

powers of the Sea-Blues, by luring the merchants
into alliance, either by marriage or by bribery. In
this they had not had much success; the difference
between the two Factions was too great; it was the
difference between intellect and custom, between
which there must be war, if a State be ever to be
better than a farmyard.

It is generally held by the Sea-Blues that the
Dinner-Greens were a dying aristocracy. Certainly
the Sea-Blues were the growing, advancing Faction: their interests lay eastward, in Lesser Asia
and in Egypt, where prosperity marched with
splendour. In the western provinces, where the
Dinner-Greens ruled with feudal power and lack
of light, there was only the memory of splendour,
or the markedly declining splendour of a few palaces among the beggary and slavery of farms
under the thumb or the thumb-screw of the agents
of the palace lords.

The rebellion of which I have to tell ended the
excessive fury of Faction in The City. The young
people of to-day cannot understand the passions of
those times. Even now, I write with the indignation of a Sea-Blue who finds it hard to believe that
Dinner-Green iniquity should so long have pre-
vailed.

Yet sometimes, in calmer moments, to-day, I
feel that perhaps something like a principle was
contended for by that Faction; and that even if it

were a wrong principle, and against the good of
The City and the Empire, it was held, and pas-
sionately defended.

Much must always be said for a class with leisure, a class above petty greed, with noble ideals,
great general culture, knowledge, wisdom and fine
manners, dedicated to the conduct of The State
and the enlightenment of man; and able to give to
its children the tradition and custom of these
things. I am impressed always by the Eastern tales,
which insist on the value of good birth, and make
the wise, heroic and virtuous prince always the
son of one something of the same kind, if in a less
degree. But when the class with leisure loses its
ideals and opposes general culture, what then?

We of the Sea-Blues were for a century contest-
ing with these people for an administration based
not on prerogative of any sort, but on efficiency
and proven fitness. We knew, and I, from harsh
experience know, how savagely and stupidly we
were opposed by those who had once held by
merit, and now hoped to hold by none.

I admit at once, that Justinus, the founder of
our Dynasty, had no shadow of right to the throne;
he snatched the crown by fraud and held it by
force. He was not a Ruler; he was a soldier of fortune, and none dared try conclusions with him,
without tasting his soldiery. His nephew, Justinian, was not only a Ruler, but a reformer; and to

have a reformer on the throne, with no shadow of right to the crown, save the fact that he was nephew to the power-snatcher, was more than the great ones of the Dinner-Greens could endure.

Justinian was a scholar, profoundly learned in Theology, and in Law; this, in itself, was appalling to a class, which boasted of its ignorance and daily, loudly spoke its contempt for scholars and thinkers. His Empress, the Lady Theodora, had been for some years a dancer in the Ballet. Yet the great of the Dinner-Greens, holding hereditary Palace offices, had to treat these two as Emperor and Empress. You may imagine with what grudging they did their service. They called Justinian "the Usurper", and his Empress "the Scarlet Woman". I saw them from time to time, in the early days, white with fury, and with twitching lips, men and women alike, at some Court Ceremony, at which they had to attend, kneeling, awaiting the Imperial signal, and then retiring backwards from them, bowing or curtseying at every second step. Naturally, from the first, the Imperial Pair set themselves to abolish such hereditary offices; some twenty of the great were removed from their place at the Centre. You may judge, if they thought this better than the loathed subservience; they raged at it.

Much of the bitterness of the Dinner-Greens towards their opponents must have sprung from the knowledge that they themselves were declining. In the past, they had owned and ruled; to some extent, they still owned; and all believed that they ought still to be ruling, from the fact that they had once ruled. But it was plain to them that they were fading and the Sea-Blues were growing. This was a matter which could be proved. It was fifty years since any of the Dinner-Green families had produced even a tenth-rate administrator, speaker, churchman or judge; and a hundred years since it had produced even a trifling book. It had once been said, that the aristocrats had fine manners and beautiful features. If this were true, they had lost their manners; their insolence was proverbial. They had lost their looks; the men looked brutish or foolish and the women ill-tempered. Style is a matter of selection; when castes cease to grow it becomes a matter of exclusion. These people had become exclusive; all feeling for style had gone from them; they had long ceased to build, to read or to collect. Their one interest and excitement was chariot-racing; they lived for this; all their energy and all their fortunes were devoted to this; men and women alike lived for the Hippodrome and its insanity. It may seem impossible to this generation, but it was clear to mine, that their vision of a perfect State was their own caste preeminent, holding all power and dispensing all place, and a slave multitude below them, gasping for their one glimpse of happiness, the Hippo-drome, the delight of their masters.

Since all thought necessarily condemned them and their order, they strove with all their power to stifle thought. They had always in their pay, and subject to their suggestion, a great number of chaplains, speakers and school-masters, who preached their doctrines and exalted them. They had always in their pay or in their power not only their country-tenants and retainers, but the thou-sands of City-dwellers, who lived in the houses they owned and served in the many industries which they controlled. They employed great num-bers of house-agents, rent-collectors, produce-mer-chants, wine-sellers, tallow and timber agents, oil-sellers, whose votes were made to go as they, the bread-dispensers, wished. It was a part of the po-litical creed of these people, that the majority of the State should be humbly subservient to the few. The few, in return, after checking and nulli-fying any system of public teaching permitted, allowed to the many the spectacle of wealth at leisure. The many were allowed to have the spec-tacle of the Races at the Hippodrome, when the few flaunted the extravagance of costume, jewelry and waste before all eyes. They had among their supporters, the dealers in costumes, silks, furs and jewels, the traders in cosmetics, hair-dyes, and methods of the toilet, the providers of costly and

outlandish foods and drinks, and they held also, as
their chief key to popularity, the business of the
Chariot-Race. They, whose select Clubs, the Charioteers and the Quadriga, gave laws to the Hippodrome, were the dispensers of the monstrous folly
of the Race Weeks; they had behind them the
jockeys, drivers, grooms and charioteers, all the
touts, the sporting publicans, the gamesters, race-
goers and betting-men; and through these, the
main teachers of their gospels, their doctrines
reached the multitude. It may seem strange to
you, but they had constantly at work public speakers whose task it was to excite interest in the
Races, and to condemn all those who protested
against the folly, madness, waste and misery caused
by betting, and against the barbaric cruelty of the
Races themselves, by which in every year, many
fine horses and daring men were killed. Few
minded the death of the men, perhaps, they were
seldom remarkable for intelligence, but the killing of so many horses refuted the plea, that only
by Racing could the breed of horses be maintained.

Though they were a dying stock, withering at
the top, ceasing to produce brains, as castes do,
they still had enormous power; from the first, they
pitted this power, their wealth and the weight of
centuries of custom, against Justinian, who was
determined to remake the outworn frame of things.

Centuries of custom had given this Dinner-Green or feudal faction the control of the Army and its appointments. It had been a shock to them, when Justinus, who had been a private soldier, became Emperor. Justinus, however, had not been a reformer, and had left the Army much as he found it. Justinian had begun a reform of the Army, by giving high command to a young man of humble birth, Belisarius, whom he made Count. The rage of the Dinner-Greens at this appointment provoked the long machinations which led to The Persian War.

There can be little doubt that our War with Persia was contrived by members of the Dinner-Green Faction, in the ambassadorial service, in order to give importance to their caste, to ruin the Sea-Blues, and to cause discontent in The City, and anger against Justinian. Being more than a thousand miles from The City, these ambassadors were able to direct matters much as they chose, against the wishes of the Emperor. They provoked the Persian King by repeated treasons until war began. The outbreak of war, though expected by the Dinner-Greens in The City, came as a shock to Justinian, who had been hoping and working for peace. It became much more of a shock, when he learned the condition of the Army, now wanted on the Persian frontier and for the defence of Antioch and the splendid cities near it. He sent

Count Belisarius to command there: and then began to discover what he had to command.

It is difficult for anyone who has not seen it to understand the incompetence of the Dinner-Green professional soldiers in all matters outside a drill-ground. They have no imagination, no foresight, no professional scholarship, no thought of any war save the last but two, and all the obstinacy of mules in resenting and refusing wise suggestion. To all these defects they added a dishonesty beyond parallel, which in its cumulative effects was nearly fatal to us. For years, they had caused to be voted huge sums from taxation for the arming and equipping of our troops and the furnishing of the magazines along the coasts of Karamania. These sums, by subtle systems of peculation, went to their own pockets or to the contractors in their interest. From time to time in the Senate, the generals in charge of our Department for Strategy would rise up and say that our armed strength was the just terror of all possible enemies, and that the Army was never better-equipped nor readier for anything that it might be called upon to do. Shortly before the war began, the head of this Department said that war was most unlikely, since he knew, from unimpeachable sources, that the Persian Army was in no condition to take the field, that its generals were opposed to their King and had declared that they would never take arms against the Empire. "Let these idle chatterers, who talk of a Persian War," he said, "sleep in peace. Though it is not in the public interest to declare what steps are being taken, I may say that we are prepared against every possible eventuality, even (though the chatterers may doubt it) for peace." Many Senators of his party laughed at this and applauded him. Then the war began with a swift advance of the Persians against our outposts and a terrible dread, that Antioch might fall. Ah, then it was that Justinian learned the kind of Army that existed. It was not an Army at all; it was not even a framework of an Army. It was not a case of troops without weapons, or without modern weapons; it was a case of corruption in high place, such as we had never suspected, of shadow regiments, which did not exist, but yet drew rations and pay and the money for equipment; of shadow arsenals, not yet built, but drawing money for building; of shadow stores, for which receipts existed, but which did not exist and never had existed; of shadow magazines from which goods by the thousand tons had disappeared. When put to the test, the Department for Strategy was shewn to be such a fraud as has seldom been known even in that Department.

Now a Persian War immediately threatened the interests and possessions of the greatest of the Sea-Blues, the traders to the East. They had dreaded a war with Persia, but their enemies had provoked one. Now they set forth such a cry, of Antioch and the seaboard cities being in peril, that The City was stirred as never before. The cry "Save Antioch" was on every lip.

Whatever men could be found were hurried into ships and sent to the East; usually footmen, to fight cavalry, and spearmen, to fight archers, under every conceivable disadvantage which the stupid can inflict upon the brave. Governments have always the means of keeping the truth from the public; but the wives of ministers and trusted officers always talk; something of the truth became known, and the bitterness of the judgment fell, not upon the old generals responsible, but upon Justinian, who had trusted them and believed their knightly words. Luckily for us, he had placed in command in the East his young friend, The Count, Belisarius, who contrived to save us from disaster. The War drained away from The City every soldier who could be found; all who were under the colours went; all the reservists went; then, all the pensioners. Soon, it was necessary to send the trained men of the Harbour Guards, the naval training squadrons, the old Naval men who served in the Customs; then the force of City watchmen, the police; and lastly the Palace Guards, the Sardicans, the clansmen of the Emperor. All these men, all who were competent to keep the peace within The City, went. Their places were taken by those who could be spared from other work, such as the building and equipping of ships; the growth of food, and the making of weapons; for we had no weapons. These men of the replacements were by no means the trusty ones whose places they took. Many of them were ill-disposed to the Dynasty; many of them loathed the war, and resented being called to take a part in it; many were idle, subversive fellows, who were determined to avenge themselves upon the government for enslaving them by doing as little as they could for as much as they could get. These, as long as they had comfortable quarters and free rations, did not much mind how long the war lasted. It was said in the Palace that after these men came into the garrison, it took an entire squad to do in a morning what a file had done in an hour. As always happens in a war, the public services became neglected; the mails and supply services were much pillaged by petty thieves, the streets were less well cleaned; and less well lit at night; crime of all sorts increased, owing to the worsening of the police service; the schools became less effective; many of the best masters joined the army, and the boys were free to play truant, and join gangs. The citizens had ample cause for complaint, and uttered their complaint against Justinian.

When the Empire was committed to the Persian War, and The City defences had been stripped of men so that Antioch might be held, the possibility of danger from the great nobles, the landowning Dinner-Green Senators, was ever present in the mind of Justinian. Those lords had a military power of their own, in addition to their immense power of swaying public opinion. Most of them had country houses or palaces within forty miles of The City; both there and on their main properties further to the west, they maintained cavalry of a sort among their retainers. These irregular horse-troops had been discouraged by Justinus, but had never been forbidden. They existed, and from just before the Persian War until the time of the rebellion they had been much enlarged and much exercised, on the plea, that The Empire needed them or would need them. Few if any of these horsemen were allowed by their masters to go to the war; the great lords drilled and equipped them and in some cases contrived to get grants from the Treasury for them, but kept the men and their horses and equipment at home, though on a war-footing as it is called, ready to move, with their carts and forage. There were some three or four thousand drilled and equipped horsemen within fifty miles of The City, all of them in the pay and the service of one or other of these feudal chiefs, to whom they sometimes owed a clansman's devotion, but more generally a slave's obedience.

Among these lords was one Protarchus who owned many vineyards, and had great wealth from a particular kind of cheap spirit much loved by the multitude. He had been a cavalry officer as a young man, but had been removed from command by Justinus for incompetence (or rather insolent disobedience). He had a bitter loathing for the Dynasty for this reason. He was one of the richest and therefore one of the most powerful of the racing party. He had been given command of three or four squadrons of the irregular cavalry mentioned above, and took great interest in it, spent much money upon it, and contrived to bring the squadrons frequently together for training. This was known to Justinian, who knew also that these cavalry were never offered to the Empire for the Persian War, but retained on the western estates: "As a first line of defence in case of invasion." Protarchus was of course a Senator, though he seldom attended. He was a fair horseman, with a pale rather fat face, no general intelligence, no personal ambition, a great dislike of thought and thinkers, and the fixed belief that anyone who differed from him, or judged him, was one of these cranks, one of these public dangers who needed the strong hand.

Though the Dinner-Green Faction and the Persian War were great causes of the Rebellion, there were others of some importance.

In all Empires, and in every City, there are always subversives and rebellious, who are against the community, either because they have suffered from it, or because of some perverted creed. In Byzantium, we had some of both sorts, who, together, helped the explosion, and indeed, for a time ruled the outbreak. They were men of some talent, to each of whom Faction and the War gave evil opportunity. I will mention these. Like the Dinner-Green Faction, each of them commanded a considerable force. As always happens in war, the strength of each force was not certainly known till the time came.

The most dangerous and the ablest of these men was one, Bessus, who had been a subaltern in the Army in the brief campaign in the East under Justinus. He had been drummed out of the Army for theft, and had since that time been a wine-merchant's traveller and a ward-politician, getting a good deal of rather dirty money and always aiming to destroy the civilisation which had disgraced him. He had a real talent for soldiering, and undoubtedly believed that he was a great military genius, whom jealousy had robbed of the chance of glory. He bore some slight facial resemblance to the face on the coins of Julius Cæsar; and to make this clear, he clipped his hair and went

clean-shaven at a time when men wore their hair
and beards long.

.Some years before the Persian War, he started
(with much backing from the Dinner-Greens)
what he called The Youth Movement in Byzantium. He claimed that this was to provide gymnas-
tic training for poor lads; but The City learned,
too late, that its real aim was to provide a revolutionary party with a strong force of well-trained,
drilled, armed, devoted fanatics, each under
twenty-five, and all certain that Justinian had kept
them from Liberty, and that if a man had not Liberty he had better die.

Next in importance to Bessus was his friend
Rufinus, a dapper little lawyer, a most ready
speaker, with much power over an audience. Bessus was swayed by the wish to shew himself a great
soldier. Rufinus had no personal ambition; he was
what we called "a pure revolutionary". He wanted
to destroy any system which existed, but had no
very clear view of what was to happen next, except
that selfless Virtue (such as his) would confer Liberty everywhere.

A third man, the City-agent for one of the lords,
a ruffian named Teraunon, who had been in a
money-lending business with Rufinus, was important in the Rising, because he controlled the Race-
Course gangs, of boxers, criminals and thieves,
employed by the book-makers. He had a coarse

power as a speaker. He came into the Rising for greed; he was in it for plunder; and tried to get out of it to save his neck.

These three were not intelligent, but each had much energy in affairs.

I have now mentioned the main forces of the Rising which found their chance on that fatal New Year's Day. There was an aristocratic force, of the Dinner-Greens, eager for the destruction of Justinian; this force we overrated; there was the revolutionary force of Bessus, which we underrated; and there was also the cold, Satanist, anarchic power of Rufinus, leagued, now with the destruction dear to Bessus, now with the greed which swayed Teraunon. Not one of these three forces would have a chance of making head, but for the Persian War and the power which this gave to some, and the weakness it revealed to others.

In all wars, personal liberties become restrained and happy enjoyments difficult; the lie becomes extremely powerful, and adroit scoundrels find it easy to plunder the citizen on some plea or another.

The western lords, thinking that they might make much profit in the troubles, by putting up the prices of corn and meat, created a scarcity by withholding supplies. The prices rose; and those who suffered most blamed Justinian. He dealt firmly with these profit-makers, by insisting on sworn returns of all holdings of corn and cattle,

and the regular sending of a proportion from each
holding to The City's markets. This insistence on
returns was bitterly resented by the lords, who
swore that no upstart Sardican should examine
into their private possessions. They set going a
paid slandering of Justinian throughout all The
City; their speakers said that he had vowed to end
all liberty by prying into the private lives of all
the citizens; this was believed. He was bitterly
blamed by everybody.

At this point, a year ended. On the New Year's
Day, exactly one year before the rebellion broke
out, the fire which set going the blaze became the
Chief Magistrate for the Year. John of Cappadocia became Epargos. John made the rebellion certain. When the Dinner-Green lords withheld supplies of corn and meat, John of Cappadocia said
that he would make them mourn that they had
ever tried to milk the citizens; he would milk
them instead.

He was a turbulent, fierce, full-blooded greedy
man, quite illiterate, but of a rough practical wisdom and capacity, without any tinge of softness or
delicacy. He hated the Dinner-Greens; and welcomed their opposition. "Now I will break those
racers and chasers," he said. "When a man hits me
on the cheek, I will hit him on the other cheek
also, as Scripture says. They'll be sorry for their
short-sightedness before many days are past."

He ran through a short bill in the Committee of the Senate, and had it signed by Justinian. This Bill, which was called, "An act to ensure supply", gave him almost unlimited power.

In time of war, most ruling powers become absolute; the herd gives up everything in the hope of safety. In the mess in which the Empire stood when John came into office, he was a very present help in trouble.

He had no religion except a hatred of the Dinner-Greens, or, shall we say, of pretence. He disbelieved in birth and privilege; he had neither himself; he liked a man to stand by some power in himself. He was very handsome in a coarse, brutal bullying way. At that time, he was in early middle age. He had dark, untidy, abundant, very beautiful hair; fierce, swift eyes, which cocked up at his opponent as it were from sideways. He had high colour, and an extraordinary mouth, at first sight loose and relishing, with a sneer on it, and then, on a longer view, with a hard, cruel tightness, without any evidence of mercy. He had a rough humour with subordinates, which made him popular with them; he was very civil always to women, quite charming in his courtesy to all servants, as long as things went well. His servants adored him, but were so terrified of him that they took good care to make things go well. One young Dinner-Green, who was in the Office of the Chief

Magistrate, thought that he might suggest to John, when assuming office, how things should be done. "The young cub's pelt went into the gutter," John said. No other Permanent Official took any liberty after that. He soon shewed each Permanent Official what work meant under him. He began by lengthening the hours of daily labour at all public offices by four hours in each day, for the old rate of pay; he insisted that the hours should be worked and observed; he was there to see to it, and vengeance fell on any who failed. He himself was a worker. He worked sixteen hours a day, seeing men, examining, blaming, encouraging, rewarding; going through piles of reports, seeing at once any wanting thing, and exacting it before anyone slept. After the sixteen hours, which he passed with hardly any food, save a crust or two of burnt bread and a drink or two of water, he went to his main delight, his dinner. He ate like a wild beast, gurgling with greed, shovelling coarse and delicate dishes into his mouth with a joy which made men sick. Then he drank till he was drunk, and so to bed, unless work were very pressing, in which case he took disgusting measures to clear his head, and made shift to do it. His instinct was so sure that even when three parts drunk his decision was likely to be sound.

This terrible force, licking his lips at the prospect, set forth to punish the Dinner-Greens for trying to cause a scarcity. He sent his valuers down upon some of them. Their goods were minutely examined and assessed, then mulcted, then distrained upon, at last seized, without shadow of right, on John's own reading of his own Edict. Then having pillaged much goods he turned upon those of the Party whom he disliked. These he dragged up for examination, and bullied and blackmailed, now on some plea, that he suspected a plot, now, because they were Dinner-Greens, and then, again, because if they were not plotting, they might be later. He did appalling things by blackmail, brutality and theft; but always under his Edict and with the excuse that we were at war. It was his plea, that the Empire was in danger. In a way, it was; but his aim was to make it in no danger from the Dinner-Green Faction. "I'll draw the teeth of those bright birds," he said. "Their snorty women'll know better another time." He issued another Edict, which forbade women to wear jewels in public, to spend more than fifty pieces in the year on clothes, to wear clothes which might in any way be held to resemble the clothes of men, to dye their finger-nails, and to coiff their hair in the expensive styles in use. No man did more to outrage feeling than John in his magistracy. You could feel the silent rage of his victims as you walked in the streets.

A month before John's year of office ended, that

is, at the beginning of December, the Naval Guards, going their rounds at night, came upon a man in the timber-stacks in Fifth Ward, near the Harbour. He had no business there, and could not explain his presence. He had upon him flints, steel, tinder, and a gourd full of inflammable gums. There was little doubt, that he was there to fire our Naval timber, seasoning there. Whether he was in the pay of the Persians or of some subversive body was never known; he was a staunch fellow, who would not tell. John decided that he was a traitor in the pay of the Dinner-Greens; proclaimed that he was such, and had him executed at once, as "a treacherous Dinner-Green, trying to ruin his Country". This, of course, shocked the Dinner-Greens into protest. They sent speakers through The City, crying that the harmless citizen Paulos, caught on his way home from work by ruffian gangs of the Sea-Blues, had been falsely accused and judicially murdered by the usurping Faction.

Now John had committed so many acts of injustice that many believed these speakers: it was astonishing how great an effect they had. Their employers, seeing this, went further. They hired from one of the music-halls an actress with a face of pathetic beauty. They paraded this woman through the streets upon a cart, with two hired babies, and placards saying that here were the widow and fatherless babes of the new victim of the Imperial tyranny, so foully done to death. Paulos, as far as I could learn, had neither wife nor lawful child, being one of the robuster scoundrels of the Sixth Ward, the breeding ground of such. The effect of this parade was very great and also profitable; they made collections in the streets, "for the widow and poor little fatherless babes", to which, what from weakness and threats, many people contributed, even large sums. Seeing the effect of this parade, the Dinner-Greens thought fit to appeal to the Emperor at his Christmas alms-giving in the Hippodrome. It is the custom at these alms-givings for the Emperor to stand, holding forth the Sacred Elements, and cry aloud that by the help of the Holy Things he will do Charity and Justice. On this occasion, he made his cry and was about to give his alms to the poor gathered below his throne, when the spokesman of the Dinner-Greens, thrusting forward very rudely, demanded justice for the Green Party, which as he claimed had no justice, but tyranny and unright. The Imperial Answerer rebuked this spokesman, and ordered his followers to disperse. Instead, they shouted for justice, and taunted the Emperor with the murder of Paulos. The unseemly display was checked by the Emperor's ig-

noring of the noise and proceeding with the alms-
giving. A few men were arrested later and fined
for disorderly conduct.

It may be said, that this was the first movement
of the rebellion. We, in the Palace, were not
alarmed by the state of The City. We knew, of
course, that John had done many outrageous
things as Chief Magistrate; but for one thing, we
had been at war, and for another his year was almost at an end, in a week, he would be out of
office, and that cause of dispute would be gone.
The Persian War was at an end; that cause of bitterness was done. Two things made me uneasy at
that time; one, the slowness with which our Army,
containing the bulk of the City police force, was
returning from the East; and secondly, the incompetence and slackness of the citizen police force
which was taking its place. Crime was more frequent than it had been. However, it was winter-
time, when crime is less than in the summer; it was
fine weather, when the watch was usually better
kept than in times of storm; it was also the Christmas time, when good feeling is at its height. If I felt
uneasy, when I thought how defenceless The City
was, the comfort at once came. "Well, the Army
advanced guards are at Smyrna, and by this time
have doubtless pushed on." After the little dis-
turbance at the alms-giving, I urged the Emperor to signal the advanced guard to press their

march to The City. The signals were sent, acknowledged, and as we supposed, were obeyed. Unfortunately, some of the senior officers, who had been bidden to a civic feast in Smyrna, delayed their march till after the feast. As we believed that they had marched, I can say truthfully, that no one in the Palace or in The City expected any trouble. It was my task to try to keep a finger on The City's pulse, and to let the Emperor know what was being thought and said. For a day or two after Christmas, the mind of The City was certainly better than it had been. Christmas had been a great healer of bitterness; the Church had striven to give people Hope and Peace; all were delighted, that the war was over and that John was going out of office. I would have sworn, that a new era of joy and brotherhood was about to set in. Then John, just before his teeth were drawn, did a thing which nearly ruined City, Dynasty and civilised life; and all for a petty tyranny which his drunken frenzy turned into a monstrous crime.

Christmas comes at the end of the long Fast of Advent; in The City, it always comes with rejoicing, feasting, good cheer, and more than the usual amount of drunkenness. Two days after this Christmas, some youths of the Sixth Ward, being rather drunk, went on a foray into Fifth Ward and smashed a few windows. Christmas week hardly ever passed at that time without some little raid of

the sort; usually Fifth Ward was the sinner, rather
than the sufferer. John, for some reason, chose to
take this foray as a personal insult from the
Dinner-Greens, and as a sign, that there was sedition in The City. Most of the wine-shops in The
City were at that time owned or controlled by the
western lords who owned the vineyards. John at
once gave the order that all wine-shops in The
City till further notice should shut at six in the
evening instead of nine. The amateur police force
welcomed the order, for it lessened their work
and their anxiety; but it was a harsh and tyran-
nous order, which roused intense indignation. It
was, indeed, a crowning injustice, that all the
users of the wine-shops should be shut from their
evening solace, while John in the Magistrate's Palace made himself nightly drunk. For the first
night, they hardly believed, that such an order
had been made, or could be enforced. On the next
night, when they knew that it was enforced, a
number of lads gathered outside John's Palace
and hooted him. John was out at some feast at the
time, but he heard of their coming. They had
been orderly enough; they had hooted and passed
on; but he knew very well that they would come
to him again the next night.

The next night, being the last night of the year,
the last night of his office, he made ready a special
guard for his Palace and lay in wait. A great many

young men of both Factions had long before
planned to make merry on the last night of the
year; young men invariably do. John's Edict made
all their parties impossible. These lads then,
thoughtlessly, noisily, but without real malice,
gathered together almost naturally; for what can
be more natural to youth, than to protest against
one of the inhibitions of age? They gathered outside the Epargos' House, they plucked up the
railings, they broke a few windows, they made
cat-calls, and invited John to come out and be
tossed in a blanket. John was in the savage state of
drunkenness which always made intense his love
of action. He called his guards, and at once bru-
tally and fiercely with clubs and short swords set
about these rioters, as he called them, broke them
into utter disorder, killed three, sadly wounded
many, and seized a dozen, whom he was pleased to
call the ring-leaders. These he at once sent over the
Harbour, to the terrible criminal prison called
Death-Bed-Jail, where condemned criminals are
kept before execution. All these ring-leaders were
lads of about twenty, students and so forth, of
both Factions, and usually of good family and
some learning.

It was about midnight when this fight took
place; it may have been one in the morning of
New Year's Day when the prisoners were shut into
the Jail. It is well known that the Chief Magistrate

holds office until sunset on New Year's Day. John
had some fifteen hours of power still before him.
In his drunken fury, he swore that these young
men should be made examples of. He was tireless
and implacable when roused; he seemed to need
no sleep. He at once sat in judgment upon these
lads, and put each one through a searching examination. Seven of his dozen were the sons of rich
or well-to-do merchants, builders and so forth; all
these seven he mulcted in great sums and sent
back to the condemned cells till the fines could be
paid. Five of the lads, whose parents were poorer,
or who were without rich relations able to pay
ransom, he condemned to die. Three of these were
of the Green, two of the Blue Faction. The harsh-
ness of such sentences would have been extreme at
any time; but to treat lads with such severity, was
a thing unheard of. Some of these twelve were
students at the University, and two of them were
designed for the priesthood.

By about four in the morning his sentence was
passed on the unfortunates, and order given for
the execution.

All this took place at the Jail, across the Harbour away from The City, in the quarter nick-
named Golgotha. It may be, that John thought
that in that remote suburb the executions could
be done before the citizens had word of them. In
this he was mistaken. Youth is a time of close com-

panionship. The friends of the arrested lads contrived to follow their friends to the Jail gates, and
hung about outside until they learned what was
going to be done to them. As soon as the appalling
truth was known, these lads spread the news. They
got back across the Harbour to The City, roused
the parents and friends of the condemned, and, all
unpractised as they were, spoke with the sincerity
of their love and terror to all the citizens. The
news ran through the town; work was not thought
of. The news stunned the citizens at first, but by
an hour after daylight there was frantic activity.
John had expected a throng or rabble at the Jail,
and had suspended or ordered to be suspended all
the public ferry-boats across the Harbour. In spite
of the prohibition, many people, relatives and
friends of the condemned, did contrive to cross
the water. The Clergy of the entire City were besieged; they were besought to go to the Patriarch
to urge him to go at once to the Emperor. One of
the first results of the news was to end all Faction
utterly throughout The City: the Factions worked
as one against the atrocity. But with all the going
and coming, meeting and debating what could be
done to save the lads, much precious time was
lost; the vital time was lost. The Patriarch went
to see John at the Epargos' official residence. John
was not there; he had just gone into the Palace.
The Patriarch hurried to the Palace, and the ways

leading to the Palace were crowded. Unfortu-
nately, The Count Belisarius, the leader of the
Army, was at that moment arriving from Persia.
Word of this had got about, and many people
were moving down to the waterside to see his
ships come in. The Emperor, the Empress and the
Palace staff had also gone to meet The Count. The
Patriarch did not reach the Emperor in time.

He could not have been in time in any case;
John was determined to have his victims dead before any suppliants could appeal. Before he left
the Death-Bed-Jail, he ordered that the executions
should be done early "for military necessity". The
condemned lads found that they were to die without any possibility of farewell, without any hope
of appeal, such as is granted even to murderers;
nay, even without the chance of fitting preparation and religious solace. They were to die, so that
they would be dead before any word of their case
might reach authority.

For this reason, while many in the City thronged
to welcome the victorious Count, while the bells
rang, the colours floated and the citizens rejoiced
in a New Year coming-in with Peace; while the
Emperor waited on the wharf with his Chief Magistrate beside him, that Magistrate's victims were
led out to die.

Now it was my duty later, to find out and to report what happened at that scene. I have talked

with some who were there; and all agree, that all there, even the guards and men of death, were shocked at the brutal cruelty of the sentences on lads so young. Still, citizens are usually cowed by even the appearance of law. They stood, cowed, watching, and would have watched until the end, had not a monk, a fine fellow, shewed a real religious feeling.

It had chanced, that some word of the case reached the Abbot of a monastery on The City side of the harbour, almost opposite the Jail. He was not told the particulars, only that some men had been condemned to death and were to die without religious preparation. I may add, that even this news came to him late. He could not believe the news, but the very thought was so shocking to him, that he at once sent three of his monks to the Jail, to enquire, with orders that they should insist, that the victims should have ghostly help. These monks were the real beginners of the rebellion. Three of the victims were dead, when they reached the scene, but at the outcry of the monks the crowd stirred, the last two victims cried aloud, and the leader of the monks thrusting to their side holding his cross above them, defied the guards. The boatmen who had brought the monks across the Harbour instantly cut the lads' bonds; and as instantly the crowd saw its chance and interfered. A man shouted "Out 'em, boys", and an attack

began. Women flung themselves down and tripped
up the guards or plucked their feet from under
them. Anyone who even looked like a jailer was
set upon. The survivors of the guards swore that
the monks called to the mob to kill the hangmen.
This I am sure they did not do; but the crowd
when roused was mad and the guards were attacked. They had been brutal to their victims,
now they had their brutality paid back upon
them. They had no chance at all. Nineteen were
killed or badly hurt. The rest got back into the
Jail and shut themselves in. The mob at once laid
siege to the Jail, burst into it, set free all the prisoners, killed all the jailers who had not got away,
and then set fire to the place. It was an act of spon-
taneous righteous feeling setting straight an iniquity by a wild act with frightful consequence.

The monks during all this got their two lads
safely into the boat and started to pull them across
the Harbour to Sanctuary. Long before they were
across, they saw the Jail in flames, and the whole
of The City shore black with crowds which had
gathered to attack the Jail and had found the ferries no longer running. The two saved lads were
borne in triumph to Sanctuary and made much
of. The bodies of those who had been put to death
were soon brought across the Harbour to the public place called the Lesser Fish Market. Here they
were laid in view upon the market stalls. There

was then an extraordinary scene of anguish, rage and self-dedication. These poor bodies were looked on as those of martyrs. The men of opposing Factions knelt together before them and wept and swore. Those who were present have said, that they had never seen our citizens so deeply moved by anything. The youth of the victims was the piteous thing. Speakers were there all the morning, calling the citizens to see the frightful thing done by The City's most frightful man. I suppose that one may say that the day passed in a ferment of anguish. What struck many observers was the weeping of the men. In every street, you found men weeping from rage at the iniquity of the deed, or, it may be at the folly of Faction which had prepared the way for such an iniquity. Certainly, Faction was laid aside everywhere for the much more serious evil of Rebellion. I suppose that in every upheaval of men there is one brief hour of nobility, which we may call the hour (or ten minutes) of consecration, when the end proposed seems only beautiful, and the frightful steps towards the end have neither been begun nor clearly seen in the mind. For some time on this first day the citizens were in this mood of consecration; the saving of the two lads was a holy deed; the indignation against John was righteous.

Meanwhile, the Emperor and the Government, the incoming and outgoing Officers for the Year,

the Chief Senators, the Household, the Naval and
Military Staffs, with their Guards and bands,
hardly any of whom, except John, had any least
suspicion of what had happened and was happening, were at the Point below the Acropolis, waiting in the cold sunny weather for the coming-in
of the ships with Belisarius. When at last, the
ships drew in, according to old custom, the Count
had to land, do homage to the Emperor, and ask
permission for his troops to come ashore. When
this had been granted, the troops landed. They
were, in all, just 187 men of the Count's small,
hardy, young, personal staff-officers, all under
twenty-five, and his bodyguard of picked foot, all
Barbarians, who hated and dreaded cities. These
men formed, marched past the Emperor, who
afterwards went through their ranks, and gave
decorations to those who had earned them. The
troops were then directed to the barracks in the
Palace which had been prepared for them. The
rest of the Imperial Party then went to the Palace
to the New Year's Day feast, which was always attended by very nearly a hundred of the chief men
in the Empire. It was a long, slow function, interspersed with singings by the choir of the Holy
Wisdom, and then with traditional toasts. After
this, all the guests adjourned to the Great Hall of
Council, where the outgoing officers waited till
the watchers reported sunset, when they laid down

their staffs anᴅ badges of office and the incoming
officers picked them up. All through this time
from about noon until sunset, we in the Palace
had little or no knowledge of the turmoil going on
in The City and the suburbs. After the ceremonies, when it was growing dark, the Officer of the
Day reported it all to Justinian. He asked at once
for John, meaning to question him, but John was
by this time swinishly drunk in one of the Palace
offices and quite unable to answer questions save
by odd shouts, songs and snarls. By this time, however, the right-minded among the Citizens had
come to see what must be done. All the speech-
making and talk of the day had ended, the martyrs
had been laid in state in their parish churches, the
Factions had made truce; now a great deputation,
orderly and determined, moved slowly down to
the Western Gate.

At the moment, I was waiting with some other
members of the Household for the signal of the
Emperor's approach to Evening Prayers. We were
standing in the corridor leading to the private
Chapel, when the old Chaplain, who was to take
the Service, came from the Quarters, and said:
"Some of the Citizens have come to the Western
Gate with a petition to His Majesty. You are all to
go to the gate-top, to await His Majesty."

I said: "I suppose it is about this business of the
Jail?"

He said: "It has something to do with that. Prayers will be held after the petition has been offered."

As we went up to the gate-top, I talked with one of my friends, about the nature of the petition. "They've come to demand John's head upon a charger," my friend said.

I said: "No. They know that they would never get that. They've come to ask for an amnesty for the burning of the Jail."

We went out into the clear, cold night, so frosty and fine. As we came into the court-yard, I heard a great noise outside the outer walls. There was plainly an immense crowd there; many of them talking, others still moving up, singing, and the bark of the street-orators seemingly all over the town. They had much light with them; they had brought down the flares used to light the night-markets, and the glow from these shone up above the wall-top.

When I reached the parapet, the distant sky in the west was still faintly red from the sunset, which somebody had said was memorable. The scene below the Gate-top was extraordinary. The space of the three commencing roads there was brightly lit with flares, and kept pretty clear by armed men. The sidewalks were crammed with silent people; the roads leading to the space were thick with people, and as far as I could see crowds,

with lights and banners, were surging and mill-
ing, trying to reach a point from which they could
hear the petition presented.

It was an orderly gathering, full of purpose but
in no way riotous. It was not the usual way of presenting a petition, nor the prescribed time, still a
vast crowd had asked for an audience, and we all
felt, that our Emperor was right in granting it.

Justinian appeared upon the wall in state, with
his four trumpeters blowing the Imperial call.
They blew again, for silence, when he was at what
is called the Parley Box, just over the Gate. The
mob fell silent, that is, all those near by; those further off, knowing nothing of what was going on,
made a good deal of noise still. The distant orators
kept barking just like dogs. The Emperor's Voice,
as the officer is called, spoke in the silence, asking
the men below, for what reason they had gathered
there, and saying, that the Emperor in his goodness had come there to hear what petition his people had to make.

I saw that about a dozen men had come forward
to the flares burning in the space. They were offi-
cials of the two Factions, wearing the sashes of the
colours; they looked to me to be men of the better
type of ward-politician, such as publicans, builders in a small way or book-makers of the Hippodrome. One of them, a Sea-Blue, looking upward,
called out that they had come there after great un-

happiness to ask for redress from their Emperor. They complained of the tyranny of the Epargos, John, and of his associate Tribunian, who was nothing but a tool for John's iniquity. "We ask that our Emperor remove both men from office," he cried, "and give us men with some bowels of mercy instead. And if the deeds of to-day are to be called in question, let the causers of those deeds be had in question, too." This speech was loudly cheered by the mob; the last phrase was very dear to them.

The Emperor at once spoke to his Voice, while one of the secretaries held to the light a record made of the requests. In a moment the Voice spoke to the trumpeters to blow for silence; when this had fallen, the Voice called "Hear all to what our Ruler says". He waited after this, for the crowd out of sight there somewhere had been receiving reinforcements, who were noisy and had a mind to press through their fellows into the open space near the Gate. The Voice had to cause the trumpets to blow for silence twice, while a scuffle went on down below us; some drunken men were pressing in, and those in charge there, eager to keep the meeting orderly, were trying to catch them. It was a very strange sight below the great gate, all lit up and filled with shadows by the port-fires. The darting, dancing and flitting figures made me think of a satyr play. Some men coming below me called out "Say, brother, just where's the Emperor standing?"

When there was a sort of silence, the Voice cried, that the people ought to know, that the Epargos and Counsellor changed on New Year's Day, and that this change had now been made. The silence became very marked at this. Then at a word from the Emperor, the Voice continued: "Your new Epargos is Phocas. Your new Counsellor, Basilides. If you have grievance or complaint, come before them in Court to-morrow morning, after Prayer. Be sure, that your Rulers will give you justice. Now go home, and advise your friends to do the same."

This speech had a good effect on all those just beneath the walls; so much was plain to us. The leaders spoke together for a moment; then one of them cried: "We thank His Majesty. We will be in the Court of Petition to-morrow with our charges and complaints."

I saw the leaders move towards the crowds; I heard them call aloud, that they were to appear at the Petition Court next morning, and that the gathering must now disperse. I moved along the wall, so as to try to gauge the mob's feeling about this. It was clear to me, that the mob was not satisfied. They had come in a state of great excitement, with fire and wild music, songs, and companionship; they had expected, perhaps, to see John hanged from the walls, or some such stirring scene. To wait in the cold for half an hour, expecting a pageant, and then to be told to go home and be an orderly citizen on the morrow was skinny measure. There was growling and cursing, with disputation. It was plain that they were disappointed, and by no means disposed to go. After a time, the leaders who had petitioned, called their musicians, who were halted in the background, to strike up a march, which they did. With the marching music, and a great deal of shouting, they did begin to clear two of the three roads which converge upon the Gate. I could see a movement away from the Palace, though it was painfully slow; the crowds who had not been near the Gate could not understand that it was all over. I went along the wall a little further; I could make out that there were many lights in the market and some of the loudest speakers in the world. Their loudest shouts reached my ears. Yap, yap. I even heard occasional words. "Liberty. Justice. Murder," etc. It is my belief that if people shout the first two words loud enough and long enough, they will get the third thing in liberal measure. As far as I could see, the main bodies on the two roads were moving very slowly away; at least half a dozen Ward bands were playing music; they were all playing the one tune "Fair City of my Heart"; this seemed strange to me, for usually the wards play the tunes of their colours. This fact, that the Factions had suspended war against each other, struck me as very strange. You will understand, that I was still strangely shut away from what The City was feeling.

Presently, I moved back towards the Gate. The Emperor and the other members of the Household had left the walls by this time. The space below the Gate was now pretty well filled with other citizens, who had no flares, like their predecessors, indeed, no light at all, only darkness. They were ribald, and sometimes noisy. They made cat-calls and shouted occasional insults at Emperor and Empress. I judged, that they would soon be tired of that, in such cold weather, and that then the troubles would be done. I lingered a while, and then went down into the court-yard. If I thought at all of the day, it was that things had turned out happily. John had done a frightful thing; that was ill, yet as a result of it, he would hardly be employed again; that was to the good. The Count had reached the Palace with some of his guards, that also was much to the good. The City and The Dynasty were made much safer thus. The war and the old year were over; we were beginning a new era with every hope. You will admit, that there was much to be glad for. When I reached my quarters I was astounded to find that I had been upon the walls for over two hours.

The routine of the Palace kept me busily engaged in every evening until about ten, when I went to the orderly room, to read the ward reports, which began to come in at that time from the outlying wards. As I passed through the ante-room to the orderly room, I noticed two subalterns of the Palace staff in earnest conversation, and made the mental note, that one of them seemed to be receiving a lecture. However, I went on, and found, to my astonishment, that no reports had come in from any ward. I said: "They are very late." The officer of the watch said: "The messengers cannot get through the crowd; the streets are blocked still, with these bands and petitioners. They'll be late to-night." This seemed likely enough; we were all far from suspecting that much was amiss; our fingers were quite off the pulse of The City. It should not have been so, but what with the old-time ceremonies of the New Year and the return of the Count, we had lost all touch that day.

As I passed through the ante-room, one of the two subalterns said "Lord Origen, may I have a word with you?"

"Yes, of course; what is it?"

"My friend here ought to have reported something yesterday, and hasn't."

The other, who was a nice-looking boy, much given to blushing, said: "It is like this, sir. I was in charge of a fatigue party at the little dock here yesterday. They are clearing the stores away from there. A lot of the stores are weapons, and I had them shoved into a house there. I quite meant to report it, and have a guard set, but it went out of my head; and my friend thinks a guard should be set."

The little dock was the small harbour just outside the Western Gate, beyond the open space where the speakers had just petitioned the Emperor. I knew that the storehouses were being enlarged, but had not supposed that weapons had been there. We had been so short of weapons for months, that it seemed incredible that a store had lain just under our walls; still, the Army was always giving us fresh surprises. I said: "What are the weapons? Whose house are they in?"

"They were short spears, sir, and the short swords called cattle-knives."

"How many?"

"About five hundred of each. I shoved them in the empty house of the harbour-master."

"You mean the house on the sea-wall, standing by itself?"

"Yes."

"They musn't be left there," I said. "You ought not to have put them there."

"I locked the door, sir," he said, "and the sergeant put the key in the guard-house."

"I must see about this," I said. I ran out at once to find the Captain of the West Gate. I reflected, that the weapons were probably old and past service, or men would have known about them.

As I reached the court-yard, I heard a great noise and yelling outside the West Gate, and saw the whole sky glaring from a fire. Men were hurrying from all the Palace buildings, to ask what the matter was. I found the captain of the Gate, he ran into me, on his way to report.

"These dogs have got into Probus' house," he cried, "and got all the weapons."

"Is that the harbour-master's house?" I asked.

"It was," he said. "It's a pretty bonfire now."

I ran up the steps to the wall-top; from aloft there, I looked right down on a blazing house on the sea-wall. The smoke was streaming away over the sea. The landward side of the dock was busy with flitting figures, who seemed to be rejoicing at the blaze. I asked one of the sentries, who these people were, who had sacked and burned the house. He said: "Some of the people, sir; they came in about half an hour ago."

"Did nobody try to stop them?"

"We supposed they had orders, sir."

"What, to sack and burn a house just under the Palace?"

"We supposed they had orders to go to the house, sir, or the City Watch would have interfered. The burning we supposed was an accident."

"But did nobody go from here, to try to put out the fire?"

"It isn't allowed to us, sir, to leave the Palace. We thought the Fire Services would be there, or will be there."

As I saw a party mustering below in the yard, I went down to them. The gates were opened, and we marched out, in a column of threes, with slingers to the front, being a party of the replacement guardsmen, with very little stomach for the job, as I thought. The Captain told me, that he had orders to clear away the mob, if they were lingering there, and attempt to recover the arms. I judged, that his chance of getting back any one weapon was remote, and so it proved. Our leaving the gates was signalled at once to the figures still near the dock; they slid away into the night; we met with a few boys, who said: "They had come to see the fire", or something of the sort. As to the fire, it was nearly at an end by this time; the roof had fallen, the floors had burned through; it made a dull glow on the sea-wall. We questioned one or two men whom we found beyond the dock. They knew nothing, or said they knew nothing about the sacking of the house. We made a short, and as I thought, a half-hearted exploration up some of the steep lanes there. My Captain said he would not go further, as his orders were only to clear the mob and recover the arms; as neither mob nor weapons shewed, he said, he would return to report. I urged him to push on, up into the Fourth Ward at least, so that we might at least see what was happening there; he said he would get into trouble, if he did that without orders. We therefore returned to the Palace by the ways we had come. We found perhaps a dozen people by the dock side, staring at the glow which had been Probus' house.

When I returned to the orderly room it was nearly midnight. I found some most disquieting reports from the outer wards; the City-watches had not reported for duty. As I have said, they were all replacement men, acting as police during the war. They were reported to have said, that it was no part of their duty to interfere against a righteous protest of the citizens. The City was beginning the New Year with no police force, and hardly any dependable troops.

As there was still active rebellion in The City and as the lawless ones had now abundant weapons, I went to Phocas, the incoming Præfect, to talk over plans for the steps to be taken. I heard from him that he had sent the Palace Naval Officer for the month along the Coast by a despatch-boat, to the two barracks to the west of The City, one upon the shore, the other a little inland. He was to give the soldiers orders to march at once to The City, so as to be within the walls before dawn. This would give us some seven hundred men all told, in addition to what we already had. The plan was, to overawe the Fourth and Sixth Wards, where the trouble was certain to be worst, at dawn; then, to make a house-to-house search for arms, and disarm the citizens. The police or watchmen were being persuaded. "Undoubtedly, they were very much shocked by the Beloved's (he meant John of Cappadocia) executions this morning; but we have sent to them, to shew them, that order must be maintained. They'll be back on duty by dawn, you mark my words. In a way, I'm very glad all this has happened. It will clear the air; and between you and me, it will keep the Beloved from any future employment."

I asked, if the gate-guards round the walls were to be trusted. He was surprised at my question. He said: "Certainly. The Præfect of the Walls has sent to them to warn them to be vigilant; but I see no reason to expect trouble from outside the walls; nor do I see the rebels wanting to seize the gates."

"They would get some arms," I said.

"Very few," he said. "A few old pikes, perhaps. No, no, the gates are safe."

"Have you any more news of the returning Army?"

"It's on its way, the Count says," he said. "It won't be here for a day or two. We shall have a delicate task during these next few days, making amends, such as can be made, to the Beloved's victims, and at the same time trying to prove that wrongdoing must be repressed. Still, to-morrow is a new day. Considering the fearful crime John did, we have got out of it very well, I think."

He was so confident, and took so light a view of the state of The City that I was persuaded that he was right. He thought, I remember, that the arms taken at Probus' house were much fewer than had been supposed or stated, and also in much worse condition. I gathered later, that Phocas did not trust me, and wilfully tried to deceive me into thinking that things were mending.

"Well, good night," he said, at last. "Before dawn, we shall have the seven companies here, and order will be established."

The seven companies, for whom we had sent, were middle-aged reservist troops called up for home service during the war. They were mostly men of The City or the suburbs. I was glad that they had been recalled. I went to bed thinking that all was well, yet wondering how the private Councils would work without the fierce, swift ruthless mind of John to put some life into decisions there. I kept thinking of the old sea-proverb:

"It's better to sail under a rogue than under a fool."

I was called at the usual time next morning, and at breakfast met the young naval officer who had been to the outlying barracks. He said that he had reached the first of them before midnight, and had found the officers away, without leave, at some country house, where there was an entertainment. He had left the order to march with the chief warrant-officer, and had then taken a guide to the inland barracks, which he had reached at two in the morning. Again, he had found the officers away (they were at the same entertainment); and here the chief warrant-officers were so drunk that they would not take the order. He had with great difficulty made the corporals rouse out the men, and had seen them start towards the City. On returning to the coast, to his despatch-boat, he had found the first contingent not yet started, but getting ready to start. He had seen them start before pushing off for the Palace. He said, that he had not believed it possible that officers would leave responsible commands for days together in this way.

On going to the orderly room for the reports, I found enough to startle and dismay. The seven companies had been met by emissaries from Bessus. In the absence of any officers, they had been

corrupted by drink and women. They had entered the City swearing never to bear arms against
their brothers, and had then joined with Bessus'
armed bands, to break open the western Jail and
set free the prisoners who were among the worst
in the Empire.

This was serious news, but it was cheerful to
what followed. A Council was called, to consider
the reports from parts of The City. These shewed
that the night had been filled with lawless acts;
the burglars and other thieves had been at their
work undisturbed by even the pretence of police.
The Fourth and Sixth Wards were up in arms,
and had broken up all the tax offices in their precincts. While the reports were being read, and before the debate upon procedure had begun, the
Captain of the Walls came down to say, that the
citizens of Fourth and Sixth Wards had come to
the Western Gate, to petition the Emperor. He
said: "They have two thousand armed men, in
very good order; and bands and a banner."

The Count said: "They can't be very eager
soldiers, or they'd have been at the war."

Justinian said: "I never refuse to hear a petition. If they will put aside their weapons, I will
hear this."

We all went once more to the wall-top over the
Western Gate. It was a bright, cold bustling morning. The City seemed in no way different from its

usual self. Up there on the wall, I could almost see into the Market. I could hear the cries of the stall-keepers there, as well as the bark of the orators. The ship- and timber-yards behind me were at work; I could hear the noises of mauls and adzes, but the chief noises came from the Market; dogs barked, sheep bleated, and men cried Butter, cheese, fresh fish, and raisins of the sun. Certainly, that part of the City's life had not stopped. Just below the wall, a company of men stood easy on their spears. They were all young men, with one white sleeve on each tunic as uniform; they were very fine young fellows; they looked determined. In front of them stood Bessus, his friend Rufinus, the big man, Teraunon, and some unknown to me. Behind the spearmen, against the houses at the back of the open space, were some hundreds of soldiers; these were the men who had thrown in their lots with the rebels; they had a look upon their faces, of fearing the results of what they had done; they were now openly mutineers. Some of them, as we could see, knew that their only chance was to fight like wild-cats for the side they had chosen; yet there was shame even on these faces. I noticed that not many of their warrant-officers were with them.

Phocas, as Præfect, spoke to the leaders of the force. He said: "It is against the laws of City and Empire to appear in arms without the commissions of our Ruler, the Emperor. I charge you, therefore, to lay aside your arms and disband your drilled men. If you have a petition to present, come, without arms, any elected five of you, to the Hall of Council, where you may present your petition and be heard."

Teraunon answered: "These citizens are a little tired of presenting petitions and being heard. They are a little tired of fine speech and then nothing being done. This time we come intending to have something done or to know the reason why. This time, we are not the subjects, but The People."

Phocas replied: "That is not true. You are no more The People than myself and my friends here. You are members of an unlawful assembly, mustered there with men whom you have lured from their duty. I have told you that if you have a petition to present, you may send five to the Hall of Council, to present it."

Bessus at this replied: "We are not here as suppliants. We are here as soldiers. We are not here to ask terms but to state them. You and your purple-stripes inside the walls there are obsolete. You are the past. We, here, young men with arms in our hands are both the Present and the Future. We have had enough of you. We are here to tell you that if you go peaceably you will be spared, as to life and some proportion of property, seeing that you are hardly capable of earning your own livings. If you prefer to defy The People you will endure The People's Justice."

The Count, whose indignation was hot within him, said to Justinian: "If I had one half-company of archers I would clear this rabble right out of it. Let me take my spearmen out and I will guarantee that the streets will be clear by noon."

Justinian did not answer. He was weighing what the Count had said, and also listening to Phocas, who was replying to Bessus, saying: "You are there as rebels and mutineers defying the laws of the community. The consequences to all of you will be shameful death by the law. Therefore, I charge you for the last time, to present a petition, if you have one, by any five elected members of your crew, and while this is being considered, if it be worthy of consideration, let all of you lay by your weapons and disperse to your homes."

At this, Rufinus stepped forward from the little group of leaders. He was a small man, very elegant, with a finicky way of waving his hands, which were white and long-fingered: "Thief-fingered," our Police Præfect called them. In his dress, he was neat; he was, as I can testify, fond of a subtle scent, not easily to be had in The City and costly, since it was made in Egypt or beyond. In repose, he looked white and nerveless. As a lawyer, he was tenth-rate, but exact. No one would have chosen him for any public office or service better than the twentieth rate. To look at, he was the man least likely to have power on an ignorant, drunken rabble. Yet this frail, pale, scented, sickly-looking creature was as terrible as a small snake. When he rose up, he was as a small snake about to strike; and all there knew it, and took heed. He had no voice, certainly no art of speech. His voice was harsh, his language mean, his accent always touched with the underbred whine of the underworld. He had however several powers of great importance to orators: he had much readiness of speech; much instinct for his audience; and courage. He answered Phocas promptly.

"The last speaker," he said, "whom I take to be the Præfect Phocas, of the administration which died of its own injustice yesterday, tells us that we are here as rebels and mutineers. From time to time, every State is at the brink of suffocation by old authorities and customs. All States die of these things. But sometimes, the moment of death is flung back by a vigorous life of Truth, Justice, Courage and Liberty, in young men who will not tamely die, choked by the dead hand of property and the incompetent woollen blanket of official-dom. If there be life in such a dying State it is the life of the young men who will rebel and mutiny. And we here claim to be not rebels and mutineers but the Life of the Empire taking wing into new glories. We here are the divine defiance which is of the nature of life itself. We claim to be the life of the State. Naturally all that you can offer us is death. We know that, my dear Phocas, and legal, but quite dead Justinian. We are here because we know it, and because we know ourselves to be alive. You offer us death. You offer to hear a petition from us if we will put by our weapons and disperse. But let us point out that we have left our homes, and taken up these weapons because we have done with petitions and do no longer appeal to anything which you may represent. We are here to tell you that your City and Empire have passed from you. We come, as City and Empire, to claim the living body of John of Cappadocia, guilty of the atrocious murder of three citizens, so that he may be rightfully tried and put to death. We demand the opening of the gates of this Palace to the soldiers of the City, and the surrender of your garrison, foully threatening the lives and liberties of The People. We order the giving up to justice of all those Senators, lords and other administrators who for these last years have taxed citizens on the plea of providing for the armies, and yet have sent those armies almost without weapons or equipment to fight the best-equipped army in the world. We demand, also, that the citizen Justinian, usurper of the purple-stripes and crown, put by those unjust gains, and give way to a People which knows no usurpation and permits no compromise. We demand these things in the name of The People, in the cause of Liberty, Justice and the holy and wronged name of Man. I, here, Rufinus, speak for these people. I say, that we grant you until one hour past noon to comply with our just demands. If you refuse them, may your blood be upon your own heads." He stepped back into the little group of leaders. Teraunon gave a signal with his hand; Bessus called out an order; the bands struck up, the waiting troops leaped up, fell-in and were at once in motion, back towards the Market. They left behind them, however, in the roads and in the houses near that western gate, a number of well-placed pickets, who were there to dispute our use of those ways into The City.

I was not present at the next scene in the rebellion. That was a private scene between The Count and the Emperor. While it took place, in one of the smaller rooms below the Gate Tower, I talked with an officer on the wall. He said: "Now you see the results of being helpless. Our garrison here is just chuckling at the defiance of those fellows."

Indeed, it was easy to see that the men of the Palace garrison were on the side of the mutineers. As they knew that the Army was on its way to The City, they were not going to fight against us, but I

judged, that they would not fight for us, and that
it would be most unwise of the Emperor to demand it. I felt our helplessness acutely. Presently,
I went into the court-yard, where I found the
Count waiting for his spearmen. I saw that he was
in a fume of rage. One of his staff, who was there,
told me, under his breath, that he had had a royal
row with Justinian. The Emperor had told him,
that it was idle to attempt to check the rebellion
without the trained men of the returning Army,
who might be in the City the next day or the day
after. The Count had said, that he would under-
take to crush these fellows and teach them a lesson
with only the two companies of his guards, backed,
if need be, by the seamen on harbour duty. "Now
is the time," he had said. "They are only a show
and a make-believe; they are trying to impose
upon you. If you let them carry it away, you will
lose every sympathiser you still have and deserve
to lose it." To this, the Emperor had said that a
little rashness then would lose The Empire. "The
City will not put me out, to put those fellows in
my place unless I give them the chance. It is gall-
ing and humiliating to wait still, under insult; but
if we wait a few hours we shall have our reward."
The Count, who was a pugnacious resolute soldier, was furious. On leaving the Emperor, he had
come down into the court-yard, and had sent to
parade his spearmen in their fighting gear, with

short spears and swords. They fell-in, and The
Count inspected them. They were superb in their
drill; they moved like one man. They looked what
they were, savage hill-warriors, who loved only
two things, killing and booty. They adored The
Count, who presently began to talk to them in
their barbaric tongue. They kindled at what he
said, their eyes gleamed and their teeth shewed;
they looked like wild beasts in sight of a meal.
The Count was a very wilful man at that time; he
was young, and presumed much upon his kinship
with the Clan of The Emperor. He ordered the
Gate to be opened, and marched his men out. He
said to those of the Household who stood near: "I
am going to teach these young clubsmen a lesson."
All this was just wild disobedience and defiance.

They went out, well skilled in war, against the
pickets, near the Palace gate. The pickets at once
fell back; nay, they disappeared, as the savages appeared. I, like the rest of the watchers of this
scene, came with the troops and saw them go. The
Count said: "I told you; they are only imposing
on you. Prick the bubble and it bursts." He gave
the order, to advance by the two roads up to the
market-place, where we did not doubt to find the
rebel headquarters and main body. Now, it was
well-known to us, that these savages are terrified
of cities. They are not used to civility of life. They
live in huts or tents, and often make vows not to

sleep under any roof save the sky for a term of years. I could see that they did not relish moving between and under walls, in this unaccustomed, devilish place. I knew too, that it was a principle of the Emperor's, that these barbarians should never be used against the citizens. However, like John the day before, the Count meant to do the thing first, and let The Emperor reproach him afterwards. We were not to do the thing at that time quite so easily. The Count sent out scouts ahead. They saw no assembled enemy in the lanes leading to the Market; but said, that the ends of the lanes were barricaded, and that the market was full of men and beasts. We went on quietly, but as the feeling in the savages rose, they began to tap their cuirasses with the blades of their javelins; this novel drum-beat was strangely affecting. Now all the lanes leading to the Market were old-fashioned narrow gulleys between houses; they twisted, so that we could not see what lay ahead and though I felt confident in The Count, I did not like the sensation of being shut in, unable to see what lay ahead and behind. Then, just as we were about to debouch upon the Market, we were attacked.

At that instant, The Count had halted, for someone in the rear, out of sight from us, had blown the private whistle-signal for a halt. He had halted, while the messenger, the cause of the sig-

nal, ran up from the rear. He brought, as you
might expect peremptory orders from the Emperor to return to the Palace at once. He was debating, whether to defy this order till he could return with victory, when the attack fell upon the
flanks of both columns from the roofs and upper
windows of the houses. At the same time, resolute
parties of Bessus' men attacked the rear of the
columns; from in front, driving down the lanes
from the markets, came terrified dogs and horses
with firebrands at their tails. From above the
heads of the columns fell fire-pots, tiles, darts and
stones; the rushing beasts upset the formations;
many of the fire-pots burst and scattered the men
with burning oil or pitch. I know that the Count
shouted to us to charge and get into the Market,
and I know that on the instant we were all envel-
oped in driving fire and smoke; some waggons of
forage in the market had caught fire and the old
houses and new booths at the Market entrance
were alight in an instant. All things were bone-
dry from the frost, and a brisk wind was blowing.
I know that we pushed on, stumbling over obsta-
cles and trip-cords, till we were in a sort of sea of
fire in the Market itself; the blaze rose up and
came at us in a billow. We could see no sort of
enemy in that confusion and burning, and I must
say that these famous savages behaved very ill and
suffered very heavily. They were not expecting

any such proof of valour. When we were in the Market, there was no getting back by the way we had come; the place was all one romping blaze. Our one way of escape was by running across the line of the advance of the fire and so getting down to the Harbour side. I must say that I was very thankful to be there.

We halted and got ourselves into order there. The Count had not done the cause any good by his impulsive attack. He had had his men shaken up and unsettled by surprise tactics in a kind of war at which they were at a disadvantage. He had in a manner forced the rebels to use fire, and was therefore responsible for the burning of those lanes up which we had advanced. His men, I am sure, did not kill or hurt any rebel, but had about a dozen killed and twenty of themselves cut, bruised and scorched. They formed up on the Harbourside, full of rage at their defeat. The Count, when he had reformed them, was all for making a detour, and attacking the Fourth Ward from the northern side of the Market. However, at this point, he received from Phocas such a message from The Emperor as made him turn back to the Palace which we entered by the Harbour postern. I believe now, that if he had made the detour, with his two companies of savages fighting mad as they were, he might have broken the rebellion before nightfall. However, the Emperor's orders were not to be trifled with. Phocas told me later, that he had never known Justinian so angry. When we entered the Palace, The Count was told to go to his quarters as soon as he had dismissed his men. Justinian would not see him for some hours, it being his rule never to see an officer or culprit while angry with him.

Some say that those lanes near the Palace would have been burned in any case, even if The Count had not made his advance. It may well be so, yet his advance was the cause of the firing. The firing was the cause of the triumph of the rebellion. It proved to the mob that the Emperor had no power to restore order; and when this was known, it brought all the rapscallions of The City into the Market to pillage. When the fire took hold, a multitude of appalling creatures, the spawn of mobbery, hungry, ragged and evil creatures in The City appeared as by magic to snatch and run away. Those who saw them say that they were all dwarfs, stunted, pock-marked, blear-eyed, tooth-less, noseless, slobber-mouthed, like crawling grabs; a more appalling set than any painter could devise for hell; the women more frightful than the men, since their greed for such things as the market offered was greater than the men's. One saw women biting at raw meat, and the corpses of plucked fowls, tearing at carcasses, bits of fish and hucksters' pies. They sacked the market, big as it was, in a very little time; and as some ran on, to attack John's Official Residence, close-by, for there were never lacking prompters to other evil, the mass stayed to break open the shops and stores behind the stalls in the market. It is always the case, that next to food, the mob long for firing, and the means of keeping warm. During the war, while ships had been used so much upon the eastern routes, few ships had come to the City with oil or wood. Bessus' speakers had been busy telling everybody, that John had laid in enormous stores of oil and wood, against the great cold, at the end of January and early February, when he would dole it out at great profit to citizens. All this stuff, the speakers said, was stored in the market; and to get this the appalling scum now fought, bit and struck at the shop doors and the cellar-gratings. Of course, in some of the warehouses, there was a fair supply of fuels; the merchants in such things always had a store of them. These were now broken into, and flung hither and yon; the bavins snatched, the oil-jars shouldered and then furiously fought for. Among the thieves, there were some of Bessus' young men, carefully trained by him in all the devilries of satanism. Some of these now set fire to merchants' stores; and it was proved later, that the fires started in three shops of oilmen and that these shops, though apart from each other, were all well to windward on the northern side of the Market-place, so that the flames would inevitably drive down on to the heaped bales, boxes, carts and other inflammable things in the Palace itself. While the fire was catching, the main drilled body attacked the Prefecture, the official house of the Epargos. This house was at the time in the hands of the builders and decorators, who were doing some necessary repairs and paintings. The Epargos, like John, the outgoing officer, was at the time housed in the Palace, as the rebels must have known perfectly well. However, with a short address from one of their speakers, a man with a big voice, who declared that the people would now execute Justice on their enemy, the young men burst into the house, smashed doors, windows, and fittings; then set fire to the paint, shavings and other mess in the deserted rooms, and had the place in a blaze. The street of the Ambassadors, as it was called, was composed of officers' houses; the Counsellor, the Church Treasury, the Roads and Ferries Office and several others, were there, in stately, big old houses, with the City dwellings of some of the richer merchants. When once the Epargos' house was well alight, nothing could save the buildings near it. Here Bessus, who was on the spot, was at once ready with evil. He sent his drilled men into house after house, with respectful word to the inhabitants, that they were City officers, fighting the fire, and that the orders of the Emperor were, that the houses should be emptied, so that the Fire Services might have no interruption. In some cases, they were refused admittance, or were repulsed, but it is extraordinary that in many cases, the owners and inhabitants of these houses gave up their dwellings to these young men, believing that their badges were those of the City Service and that in obeying they were good citizens. When once inside the houses, these young men pillaged and flung out goods, on pretence of "saving them from the fire". One who saw them has told me, that they worked with system and coolness, with such order and alacrity that anyone would have sworn that their work was beneficent. In every house to which they came, they swiftly took out what could be best sold. The more plausible among them asked the ladies of the house to bring out their jewels and other treasures, "so that we can put them under guard; for there are a lot of wild people about in all this confusion". It was a frequent sight there, in the street, two young men standing guard, seemingly, over a treasure-box beside the owners, while other young men ran in and out, bringing out furniture, pictures and raiment. Soon, the carts arranged for by Bessus, drove up; the treasure-boxes were loaded on to them and the owners were given checks of metal, in return for their boxes, with the word, that they would receive their goods on presentation of the checks at the Palace, as soon as order was restored. The carts then drove away, and took the booty to Bessus' headquarters in the Court-house in Sixth Ward. Very soon, the plundered houses broke into fire, no Fire Service could get to the scene and Ambassadors Street was blazing like the Market. The wind was rising throughout the morning, blowing steadily from a northern point, and pretty hard; after all the dry cold weather, all the houses burnt like tinder; the fire spread swiftly, more swiftly than the rebels liked, for it blew down towards the Palace, and by extraordinary fortune leaped across a narrow alley, always known as Muck-Rake Street, and caught the superstructure of offices over the treasury vaults. This alone saved the Treasury from capture and sack.

It must not be thought that this work was done by the People, or by men furious at injustice; the popular movement, to rescue men cruelly misjudged, was over; this Second Day's rebellion was the work of the revolutionary Bessus, who had for some years prepared his troops for a chance of the kind. His men were all young men, of some standing and upbringing; all could read and write; some were in City services, others were students in the Law Schools, the University, the Theological College, even; some were clerks, shop-assistants, and waiters; some worked in livery stables; very few were idle or criminal. Bessus had the wit to see that youth is reckless and revolutionary; he made it ready for a reckless and revolutionary occasion. Many of the young men of his army looked upon the whole thing as a good joke, as a trick which succeeded, and made the older and wealthier people look absurd.

That was a terrible afternoon to us in the Palace. We were shut-in, and besieged; The City was in the hands of mutineers and mobs. The Palace party had to stay within the walls, helpless, while the fire raged and the mob pillaged. It is the most frightful situation in which men can be, to be helpless, to see evil triumphant and be helpless, to see friends killed or robbed, and be helpless, to see order, law, goodness, rightness, beauty and their fruits destroyed and yet be helpless. To that state of anguish we were now reduced. We were not even strong enough to help to put out the fire. The gangs which did sally forth to try to make fire-breaks, were driven back. While the fire burned itself out, the mobs, backed by the soldiers, went on pillaging with growing boldness and ferocity. We on the Palace walls could hear the cries of the bandits and the screams of the victims. We could see the awful huddle of citizens flying across the Harbour and over the Bosphorus to safety, there to cower homeless in the cold, while their Rulers could do nothing, and the so-called People brought Liberty and Justice.

On this day, almost all the few City Police who tried to do their duty were killed, beaten or lured from their posts.

It is the custom of historians to say little or nothing about the weather at the time of great events. This, I have never been able to understand, since the weather, which profoundly affects the farmer and the sailor, blesses, afflicts and affects everybody; it is the changing scene of our play. Certainly, no sea or land war is free from the bonds of the weather; and a popular rising may be fostered or quenched by it. There followed two days, such as Byzantium had never known.

I have said that the weather was settled, fine and cold, with easterly and north-easterly winds. That night of the burning of the Market, the sky darkened, the wind freshened, blowing more directly from the north, with severe, penetrating, dry cold, and flurries of hard snow. It blew so freshly, and so cold that the Naval Picket-boats, rowing Harbour-Guard, had to cease their guard and lie up. When the morning dawned, it was so dark and forbidding, that we in the Palace could hardly read the signal-arms on the Naval Station at Sycæ. We could make out, however, that the

cold, and the north wind had delayed the advance
of our Army with snow. The signals said, that the
falls were heavy on some of the roads, so that the
advanced guards would not be with us that day,
nor the next, nor, as far as they could tell, the day
after that, since no one could tell what the drifts
were, nor what further falls might come, with the
wind as it lay. This was heavy news to us in the
Palace, to know ourselves helpless and to see ourselves flouted for possibly three full days more.
We knew well, that after two more days of mis-
rule, the People might cast us off as incompetent
to govern or to protect.

For the next two days, this grim weather held;
it was liker a visible curse upon The City than
words can describe. It was especially awful after
dark, when one went up on to the Palace walls.
From high up on the ramparts I could overlook
The City, once such a Queen, now dark and grim.
In times of Peace, her ways were bright with the
lamps at the street-corners, and in the open shops.
Sycæ, across the water, shone with myriads of
lights, and the waterways were gay with coloured
beacons and the lamps in ships. Now, all these
lights were out; the City Light-Service was not
working; indeed, the mob had smashed most of
the street lamps, in order to steal the oil. I looked
over a dark desolation, in which hardly a light
shewed, save in a few windows too high up to be

stoned easily from the roads. Anyone shewing light ran a good chance of being examined by The People, as perhaps worth robbing. The low dark heaven seemed to come down upon this desolation of building; the wind had a scream and a hooting in it; the air had a bite in it. At times, a gust would come, flinging hard little pellets of snow into the eyes. Whenever these gusts came, the draught found out some sparks or remnants of fire in the ruins of the burned-out houses; it fanned them up into flame for an instant, so that one saw the bones of the buildings which had once been homes. Sometimes, I saw the crouched figures of the thieves, prowling in the ruins for what they could find, even if that were only a little shelter with warmth in it. It was like looking out upon a city in Hell, where no spirit moved save Despair, Anger and Anguish.

It was at this point in the rising that the political strength of the Dinner-Green Faction was applied. It was late in beginning, it was clumsy in its method; but this was its moment. The truce between the Factions in the City had made the rising possible. The lords of the Dinner-Green Faction now decided that the rising must be turned to their advantage, and certainly to the suppression of the subversives, such as Bessus, before they became too strong. They were slow in beginning, for though they were soldiers, they were bad soldiers, and though they were politicians they were stupid. Still, they had among themselves an enormous, blind, political power and means of movement. This they now set going, with the double end in view; first, to put themselves in power, by using Bessus and the present discontents to get rid of Justinian; then, to get rid of Bessus and every other subversive or reforming element throughout The Empire. At this point, the Lord Protarchus came into the rebellion.

Like most men who have lived lives of great leisure Protarchus had little sense of the value of speed in times of emergency; he wrote letters to some other officers of the irregular cavalry inviting them to meet him with their men at a rendezvous late in the next day, so that they might march upon The City, to restore order by proclaiming a new Emperor of their own colour. Though there was no snow on the European side of the Straits, there was great delay among these horsemen. The frost and bitter wind made movement out of doors unpleasant to man and beast; no one was at the appointed rendezvous, nor did the horse begin to assemble in any number till the fourth morning, when under Protarchus it began a march upon The City.

Meanwhile, for those days The City was like a place under a curse. In a way, the life of the place went on. The farmers and market-gardeners brought some proportion at least of the supplies they usually sold. The Market was in ruin, of course, but they sold upon the wharves and from house to house, and in the cruel cold were not much molested by the armed gangs who ruled the City under Bessus and his friends. We, in the Palace, were really prisoners. We could of course have sallied out and been killed, but hourly we hoped for the Army to arrive, and for the rebellion to die down. The Army was coming, slowly, over the snowy trails; what signals came through shewed that they could not be with us for perhaps another three or four days. Some of us thought that before that the rebels would tire of rebellion and that their power would collapse. In this we were foolish; we did not understand the ambition in Bessus and Rufinus, nor how they were already seeking out the people on the lists of their proscription. Most of them had escaped over the water, where they were for the moment safe, but their houses were sacked and their descriptions put abroad. I remember how my heart sank in the evening of the fourth day, when one of the rebels below the Palace wall hailed me as I walked the rampart and called with derision: "We know all about your Army. We have read your signals. They can't be here for three days. Long before that we shall have cut all your throats and be sleeping in the Palace. Put on clean sheets and spread a good dinner for us."

A Revolution such as this is ever filled with conflicting hatreds. The wise Destiny alone knows what passions took part in the evils of those six days. All law was set aside, all order forcibly broken, all safety gone. The three leaders of the mob, Bessus, Rufinus and Teraunon, were for those first days the rulers of The City, and if they did not shed as much blood and sack as much booty as men feared, it was because of the fierceness of that terrible cold north wind which was even fiercer than they. That trinity of evil was divided against itself, though we in the Palace did not know it. Rufinus was proclaiming that men are naturally pure and virtuous, yet feeling that nine-tenths of the community ought to be murdered at once. He had undoubtedly a plan for reducing the population by nine-tenths, not from bloodthirstiness, not even wholly from injured vanity, but from the narrowness of a perverted and frozen mind. He had no personal ambition; he was wholly the Devil's. Bessus now saw himself not as Julius Cæsar but as Alexander the Great, a conquering King. He felt that with his adoring young men and his new recruits, the mutineers, he could march from Byzantium to China; he had had an overwhelming first success. He had now limitless personal ambition; he meant to be Emperor, and already longed for a privy purse for the rewarding of his men. He was already sending chosen bands to blackmail and bully and rob. The prisons were filled with rich men brought in to be held to ransom. Teraunon, as far as we can now learn, was terrified, that things had gone so far. He had wit enough to see that his colleagues were cleverer men than himself, that they had made use of his brutes and personal brutality, but that they would not share the fruits with him, but get rid of him soon, and finally. He was already seeking to betray his colleagues into the hands of the Dinner-Green lords who happened to be in The City.

The position of these Dinner-Greens and Senators must now be mentioned: they now set going yet another current into the flood, quite distinct from that of Protarchus. It must not be thought that the Dinner-Green lords who were in The City at the time, and who had for years past paid money to foment civil strife, were pleased at what had happened. Early in the trouble, they had decided that the time was come for a push against the dynasty; and like most of their class they were shocked to find the push made by readier hands than theirs. It began to dawn upon them during the first days that some of their number were as much hated as the dynasty, and were for the moment as helpless. Being scared for their lives they began to use all their influence, all their speakers, all their arts of catching the public, "to restore order". They had no intention of letting The City go to The People, far from it. They meant the City and the Empire to be the spoil and plaything of their own families. They now suddenly awoke to the fact that The City was in the hands of adventurers, and that it would stay in those hands unless they were quick. Unfortunately for their party, they were not used to being quick in anything. They were accustomed to leisurely lives, and to days which ended at perhaps six in each evening in a long bath followed by a long meal, and to weeks which ended on Friday night, when they reached their country houses, and did not begin again till they reached their City houses on Mondays at noon.

Nevertheless they were shocked to action. They met in much anxiety to discuss and debate. They decided that, at all costs, efforts must be made to gather a force to restore order, that is, of course, their own order. The problem before them was, how to uproot the Dynasty without fighting those who had begun the work. They decided that their best chance was to proclaim a new Emperor at once, if they could get enough of the clergy to back them. This latter part of the business was easy, but nothing could be done "at once" in that weather, with The City in such confusion, houses

shut, people fled, and the mails and posts suspended. The question who should be the new
Emperor was easily decided. They had the nephew
of the old Emperor Anastasius all ready to hand,
the man Hypatius, an Orthodox Christian, whom
many had expected to be chosen when Anastasius
died. His claims to the throne were slight, certainly; but the existing Dynasty had none save
that of snatch. Many people thought that he had
a Divine Right to the crown; that he was an impossible fool did not weigh with these, since he
cared for horseracing and employed some of the
best charioteers. More than that, he was one whom
they knew they could influence. They could rule
through him.

Their meeting was full of anxiety; some of their
friends had been murdered, and all knew themselves threatened. They had fomented sedition by
every means in their power, in their hatred of Justinian and his insistence on intelligence in officers
of State. Now that the sedition came, they found
it hostile to themselves, and the discovery was
shocking to them. They had among their party a
good many clergy, who loathed the Empress, and
her opinions, which they said were not orthodox.
What they really disliked in her was her intelligence, which always supported those wise men in
the Church whom they found hardest to suppress
and longed most to persecute. All the priests of

the party who could attend this meeting of "the Most Expensive", as they were usually called, were in one opinion, that every voice should be raised against Justinian, but always with the addition that Hypatius should be Emperor in his stead. They said that they believed that they could persuade the City even now to take Hypatius; in fact, now was the time. Every decent citizen was appalled at the result of Justinian's policies, both at home and in Persia, while all were now in horror and terror, because of the rule of the mob. Within an hour of the meeting's dispersion, they had some hundreds of preachers in the streets and squares, declaring that the evils which had come upon the City were God's Judgments for the usurpation of the throne by that murderer Justinus and his nephew Justinian. What but misery and war had come to them since the pure Hypatius had been set aside? But it was not too late. Even now the arms were raised which would sweep away the blood-guilty Usurper and his heretical wife. With that cleansing done, the God-fearing and lawful heir might succeed to his inheritance, restore true worship and give the people peace.

All people listened to priests in those days wherever they might be. These men caught the Dinner-Greens by abuse of Justinian; they caught the Sea-Blues by what they said about God's Judgment. Some of the priests were most unscrupulous, in saying, that even at that moment inside the Palace, Hypatius' party was planning to rid the City of the tyrant and raise him to the throne.

It was true, that Hypatius and his brother, Pompeius, were both in the Palace at that time; but each was as incapable, as ever, of planning anything. Justinian had felt it wiser to keep them under his eyes; and had given them both petty employment in his Household. For some years Pompeius had been Cross-Bearer in the Guard; Hypatius, the Introducer of Royal Guests. Both looked very important in their white and gold; and while they were there were not dangerous to themselves nor to the State.

Hypatius had cost the Empire a pretty penny, first and last. As a boy, as the old Emperor's nephew, he had been given high command in the Army, on the old Imperial plea that none but the imbecile should command the brave. He was now to cost the Empire dear, indeed. Pompeius I liked, and have been sorry for.

Bessus and Rufinus were quick to guess what this preaching meant; they had decided to end Justinian before any Green plot could gather head; but now, Rufinus insisted, that the Church should be taught a lesson, not to interfere in public affairs.

We, in the Palace, expected to be attacked by Bessus' army at dawn upon the morrow, and were sure that our garrison would not oppose them. We did not expect them to open the gates to the enemy, but knew that they would not fight for us. They were disloyal to the Dynasty, and furious with The Count for leading Barbarians against the citizens. They were bitterly hostile to the presence of Barbarians inside the Palace. We heard enough of what was said inside the Precincts, and what was shouted across the walls, to know how near to eruption the volcano we dwelt on was.

Now it was part of my duty to go about the City to listen to what was being said, and so to give our Ruler some image of the state of things. I went out that night, to try to learn about the coming attack. In my own mind, I had some hope that they would attack, for the walls were strong; the Barbarians were panting for revenge, and we had a fair number of faithful men; enough, as I thought, to hold the walls, and keep our traitors from opening the gates. It was a grim, lowering night, with small, dry snow gritting about. The streets were dark and dangerous. Parties of prowlers were abroad, claiming to be Friends of Liberty, but only abroad to seize and rob those whom they felt to be worth while. Not many were tempting Fate by walking that swift dark night.

It is not possible to give to a reader any sense of the horror of the streets. They were unlit, save where some bonfire or partly burnt wreck gave out a glare. They were littered and untidy, not only with the mess, which the Street-Service had failed to clear since the trouble began, but with broken glass and wood from pillaged houses. One who walked those streets had to go slowly, to listen between his steps and to tread carefully, not knowing if his next step might not be upon a body, whether of a victim or of a footpad lying with a knife. In some of the wine-shops of the political leaders there was light; all other houses were dark. Up towards the Sixth Ward there were pickets. Bessus had his army in billets there. Somewhere in the Sixth Ward in the headquarters the evil ones were debating their next course.

I had certain secret agents in The City, and three rendezvous at which I was sure of meeting them. The first two of my dens were empty. One had been burnt, one was shut up; in the third I found a man whom I could trust. He told me that from what he could learn the rebels, Bessus and Rufinus, had made their plans for dawn, or a little before dawn the next morning. I said: "I suppose they have bribed our garrison to open the Palace gates and let them in to kill the Emperor." He said: "That is to come later, of course. The first blows to-morrow are to come against the Church. They are furious against all these clergy who have been preaching against them during to-day: besides, they want money. Rufinus thinks that the Church is only a fraud practised upon the credulous. Bessus probably shares that belief, and knows that the churches will yield some pretty pickings. You may expect some martyrdoms to-morrow."

I said: "Those clergy have brought it on themselves. They have preached sedition all day: now they will die by sedition." He said: "Rufinus means much more than killing a few curates. He means to wipe out the Church as an institution. To-morrow will be a day of blood."

It was easy to give some measure of warning to the Church communities, and as it happened they were not in danger. Bessus commanded the troops, Teraunon the gangs, and neither wished to kill the clergy. Both wished for the Church's plunder; the day which followed was marked not by martyrdom but by sacrilege.

It would be hard to say how much Church treasure was taken on that day. The City was rich in old churches, and each church was rich with the gifts of centuries of devotion. No churchwarden had taken more care of the treasure than to lock it in some chest in the sacristy, for none for one moment dreamed that the people of The City would rob the Church. Our people were devout: temple-breaking was a crime unknown among us. In that one morning every parish church was robbed.

The robbery began much earlier than my friend had said! Shortly after midnight the gangs of armed men went to the churches. They did not break them open; they came to them with the keys which they had taken from the wardens and porters. With system and skill they opened every treasure-box and coffer, and took away the Holy Vessels, the candlesticks, the votive jewels and crosses and all the goldsmithery and broidery of the vestments. When day dawned, all the parish churches had been visited, and the plunder was being sorted in Bessus' headquarters. As far as I can learn, no opposition was made to this sacrilege in any church, yet the rebel speakers proclaimed that "the fosterers of superstition had murdered the representatives of The People in their enquiry into the riches of a Church vowed to poverty".

The flurries of gritting snow cleared off, like the sky, in the early morning. The day broke bright and clear with a strong cold north-east wind: it was a glorious day, or would have been, had there been peace. As it proved, it was the most frightful day which our City ever knew.

To myself, surveying the matchless scene from the ramparts that morning, it was no pleasure to see the sunshine. I knew, too well, that the bright weather would bring out the mob. Indeed, they were already out: the street-orators were barking their lies in every open space in front of me. It was as though the City were a market full of cheapjacks each bawling a false account of the shoddy he strove to sell. I could hear the occasional word "Liberty" and the frequent snarl of "blood-sucker" or "tyrant". The sentries on the wall with me were listening with all their ears to these fellows. It was easy to me to see that they were on the speakers' side, not on our side, and that we should be lucky if we saw another dawn. It seemed to me certain that the garrison would open the gates to the mob during the day.

While I was above the western gate, a party of rather drunken men and women came into the open space below me, between the burnt-out ruins and the Palace walls. They were dressed in the Easter vestments of priests: they had church-banners, crosses and censers with them. With these things, they danced a bear-dance which was in part a mockery of a Service. It may seem too low a thing to mention, yet I often think of it as typical of the rebellion: it WAS the rebellion: it was the beast in power, shewing its mind. Some of these creatures shouted "Holy Wisdom next". This threat was frightful to hear.

I remember well the shock with which it struck me. "Perhaps these people mean to attack the great church of the Holy Wisdom. But surely they would never do that: no man could be quite so

lost and fallen as to do that: the Emperor, perhaps, with all his household about him, but not
the Crown, the Flower and the Glory of the entire
Christian world, not the Church of Churches: no,
none could lay a hand on her."

That Church of the Holy Wisdom was the
greatest of the glories left to us by Constantine:
it was the Centre of the Christian Faith, unique in
beauty, like the Phœnix, and a place of pilgrimage
to all Christians in the Empire. All who cared at
all for religion had given something to it for over
a hundred years: it was holy with offering: it was
exquisite both for splendour and for peace.

I thought: "O God, they will sack the Holy
Wisdom. I must warn the Emperor of this. It may
be that we can check them. It may be that we can
turn their hearts from a crime like this." As I
went down from the wall I reflected that there was
a little-known way from the Palace to the Great
Church. The Emperor and his suite could go by a
narrow passage into a clerestory to a space in
which they could attend Services unseen. What if
rioters without or traitors within were to open up
that passage? It was a way leading into the Emperor's private apartments. It was the very way
these deadly snakes would be sure to find.

When I found Justinian and told him my fears,
he smiled and said: "Alas, it is probable, that they
will attack the Church. They have speakers in

The City now saying that I am about to destroy it. They always begin a devilry by saying that it is one which I am about to do. I have sent men to try to secure the Church doors. Let us go there now, to see how they have managed."

We went together along the corridors to the small door which opened to the Church. The door was small, rounded at the top, and made entirely of bronze. It was so narrow that two would have found it hard to go through abreast. It opened into a passage practised in the thickness of a wall. The lighting of this passage was from above, by thin sheets of alabaster or horn which admitted daylight. The passage swerved suddenly to the left, and there we were in a sort of lodge or recess in the clerestory, on the Gospel side of the Altar, looking down, unseen, upon a strange scene of order and disorder. Out of sight from us, in the apse, were members of a choir practising a chant with a precentor. He had a most beautiful voice, and gave again and again the inflection he wanted. After him the voices tried it, now in unison, now one by one, always with the droop which he tried to correct. Away on our left, workmen were shoring up the door with balks of wood. They were hammering and sawing; men were dragging up poles and beating in wedges. It was impressive to hear this uncouth noise of work, mingled with the voices trying the chant. A good many people were

in the body of the Church, moving about in a per-
turbed way, doing nothing, but doubtless thinking that they were doing much. Outside, on the
north door, there were bangings and crashes, which
told that men were trying to beat a way in. It
seemed to me unlikely that they would get that
door open. The west door was so immensely strong
that that, too, seemed safe. I had just said to the
Emperor, "It is hardly likely that they will ever
do much here," when the windows were broken
by showers of stones, and at one window I saw
heads, for some rebels had found ladders, had
climbed up and now flung in fire-pots which burst
and scattered fire on the floor. Mind, these were
the rabble: Bessus did not want to burn the
church, but to sack it. Justinian said: "If they try
fire, nothing can save the Church. We have no
water here. But we will make a bucket party.
Come with me." I followed him by another passage to the nave of the Church, where men were
rushing at the fire-pots as they fell with vestments
and banners, to smother them. The people there
were all men of religion, monks, lay-brothers,
clergy of the diocese, and lads from the priests'
training college. The choir had ceased to sing
when the fire began to fall; they, too, were helping
to check the pots as they fell. "Go on doing this,"
Justinian said. "I am going to drive those fellows
off the wall there." He turned to me and said:

"There are two hundred leather buckets in the Palace Stables. Get all the men you can find to pass those buckets in a line from the fish-pools there. Be quick."

I went out to do that. I had to get from the great Church back into the Palace, then to the Stables, then to find men. In an emergency like that you never can find men; all are already doing something. I saw many men on the ramparts; there seemed to be none on the ground. The Emperor, who moved so swiftly that all said he disappeared at will, went to rouse troops from the barracks to come round the side of the Church and kill the fire-flingers.

When I had come into the gardens-court of the Palace, I knew from the roaring that a great body of rebels was attacking the Church. In struggles in which there is any equality between the strugglers, a very slight thing will turn the scale. Often a tiny thing will suffice. It is said by some of those who watched that IF, at that moment, Belisarius with two companies of his Barbarians had sallied out upon the attackers, nay with one company, he would have routed them utterly, and broken the rebellion. He might perhaps have saved the Church, but he would not have done more; for behind the mob at the Church were all Bessus' men and at least three times their strength of other troops; the Barbarians would have been

beaten. Other observers have said that IF, instead
of sacking the Church, the rebels had attacked the
Palace, the garrison would have welcomed them,
and Justinian would have been killed. It is best to
leave all these IFs, and try to tell what happened
in moments of mad confusion, devilry and disorder. I call them moments; they seemed like
hours, and yet when you reckoned them as hours
they seemed like moments. When, in those hours
of moments, one tried to do any one thing, a hundred other things rose up to stop its doing, and to
thrust forward things to be done first. Frustration
and retardation are the enemies in war; it is the
being unable to act freely that is the curse in life.
In childhood, sickness, war and old age, all the
four curses of man, this being tied, this being unable, is the annulling thing.

For myself, my orders were to get a line of men
as bucket-passers from the fish-ponds to the
Church. I went first to the stables. After all, the
buckets were there; we should have to begin
there. When I was out in the open, running to
the stables, I saw fire and smoke driving down
upon us. When I reached the stable, the horses
were already in panic from this. The men were
trying to get them out, down to the water-side. I
told them: "Never mind the horses. The Emperor's orders are to take the buckets and try to

save the Church. Get down the buckets, and make a bucket-chain from the pools."

The men were all hot and anxious from wrestling with the horses. They were not disposed to listen to one not an officer and unknown to them. I told their officer, the Keeper of the Horse; he gave me a rough answer. I told him that if he let the Church burn it would be as much as his head was worth. At this he said: "You tell me to take buckets to save the Church. What buckets? All the buckets from here went to the fire at the harbour there, the other night, and not one has been brought back. We have to fetch the horses' drink in the men's dinner kids. Tell the Emperor that, if he asks for buckets from here."

Indeed, as that was the truth, the bucket-chain became impossible. The Horse-Keeper relented at this point; he was scared for the Church. He said: "There it is; we've no buckets here. But you might find fire-buckets on the Wharf there; only the Sea-Guards will hardly let any go from there." I thanked him, and ran on down to the Sea-Guards, to try to raise buckets and bucket-passers from among them.

In this hour of time, when perhaps the Church might have been saved IF, the Emperor went to the main barrack for Belisarius the Count, to command him to attack outside the walls. He found the barracks deserted; all the men were up on the walls at one point or another. It was a long time, before he found the Count, who had his men on the northern rampart, defending it against an attack which Bessus had put in there, to ensure a diversion while the Great Church was taken. The Emperor found that the Count had with him only his own men; our garrison soldiers were keeping far from us.

All this time, a rabble of rebels tried to force the Church's western doors. Some of the monks and singers, at the bidding of the Precentor, a young, hot-headed priest, with a pugnacious mind, manned the wall above the doors, with slings and bows. They made it impossible for the rebels to ply the battering-rams which they brought to beat their way with. These fighting religious may well have saved the Palace by their valour, for if the mob had found the passage into the Palace from the Church, as they probably would, our throats had all been cut before dark. These brave men kept the west doors; and the little north door was so small, and so very strongly built-up from within, that the rebels could not break in there. Finding the ways blocked, and dangerous; and knowing that at any moment they might be attacked by The Count's spearmen, whom they much dreaded, in any open daylight attack, the wilder youth among them brought up more fire-pots and set about flinging these through the broken lights and into the eaves and crannies. They may have thought that a few fire-pots would drive the monks from the nave; but they did not know the monks; they had to learn. The monks flung stones at the rioters, and gathered stuffs, carpetings and hangings with which to smother the fires which broke out. They saved the Church by these efforts till well on into the afternoon, when Bessus began to fear that he was beaten. He meant to conquer. He took charge of the attack on the Church, and with a great cry of "Conquer," assailed the west door. While this was being pressed with outcry and the flinging of many fire-pots, he himself, with some bold men, got up on the northern wall, and there fired the rafters. The wind was freshening at that time. The woodwork caught, the fire spread. The monks and others down below did not know what was being done till the nave was full of smoke and the roof a running judgment of fire. By the time they had learned what was happening, the evening was on them, their Church was lost beyond all possibility of saving, and their own lives were in deadly danger. In an old strange rambling building like the Church, with many corridors, passages, vaults, out-buildings and adjoining offices, there are always draughts to fan fire, lead to melt and drip, hangings, all mothed and dry, lighting up at a spark, and in all cases a want of proper light to see by. Now, in a sudden gust the fire leaped and became alive in fifty parts of the Church at once. The lathwork which held the tiles collapsed, so that the great purple tiles of Constantine came crashing into the aisles. The lead poured in a bright stream at one place, so Brother Pacomius told me. It looked, as he said, like quicksilver, and splashed into pellets which flew about and burned the monks' legs. The body of the Church filled with driving, ill-smelling smoke into which the lead and the tiles fell. In the darkness and confusion of this, the monks had to grope their ways out of the building; in doing this several lost their lives.

The firing of the Great Church was the crown of that day's devilry. When the flames rose up from its roof and the volumes of smoke shewed that nothing could save it, there was a lull in the fighting and rioting. People were stunned by the calamity and stood to watch. They made little or no effort to try to save the building and, indeed, when once it caught in the roof it was past saving. They stood and stared, some angry, that its burning kept them from the booty it might have given, some furious at the sacrilege and the loss of a building known to all as the centre of The City, and the sea-mark to all seamen coming near; others interested in the sight, and watching it as they might have watched a play; some of them glad, as

I have learned since, feeling that the worst was now past, the Church was gone; after this, they felt, the rioters would fear God's Judgment and provoke Him no further. It is possible, that even some of the leaders of the riot were a little daunted by these thoughts late that afternoon.

To the party of the Emperor, shut up in the Palace, this burning of the Church was frightful. We felt that we could never recover the City after such a disaster. Here was an Emperor shut up in his house, utterly unable to save the greatest Church in Christendom, the world's centre.

The Church burned for the rest of the day and made all that side of the Palace too hot for us. The rabble on this day took that cry of "Conquer" which had marked the firing of the Church as a war-cry. It was hooted at us from the City side of the wall. The enemy pickets and sentries hooted it at intervals throughout the rest of the time.

In the worst of that day, when the Church was glowing, and darkness was setting in, I was sent for to the Council Room, where I found The Imperial Pair, The Count, Phocas, Basilides and three Senators. Procopius, who was The Count's adviser, was there, and a Captain of the Guard, whom I had seen but did not know, a fellow of good birth and nice manners, faithful, I think, but not very gladly faithful, to the Ruling House. "Come in, Origen," The Emperor said, as I appeared. "We are waiting for you." Then as I took my seat, he turned to this Captain and said: "We are now all present. Will you tell the company what you have to report?"

The Captain stood, saluted, and began: "About twenty minutes ago an arrow was shot across the wall with this letter attached to it. It says: 'Friend, your Rulers are doomed. Do not risk brave men's lives trying to defend them. Open the gates to your friends who will well know how to be grateful, so that we may crown the rightful heirs.' On my way to bring this to His Majesty, a rebel hailed me from the street and said: 'At midnight your men are going to open the gates to us and we are going to crown Hypatius.' "

Phocas took the word here. He said: "Word was brought to me from a source which I cannot neglect that that is the policy of one party at least of these fellows. Whether it is the policy of their strongest party is another matter; I feel that many outside the walls hold very different views."

One of the Senators, a charming old man named Symmachus, said: "I went to see the burning of my house this evening. I talked with some of the men who were robbing what had not been burned; they said: 'We are going to have Hypatius for Emperor.' When I came back here, one of the stewards told me that women had been along all the east side, saying they meant to crown Hypatius, who would forgive everything and redress everything."

Justinian spoke. "That is the situation. I do not for one moment believe that Hypatius or his brother, Pompeius, are in any way aware of this plot or privy to it. But while they are here inside the Palace they are temptations to any of the garrison to open one of the gates. I think that it is fairer to them, to explain the situation to them. They do not know it. They have been in their quarters, at their duties all day; they may suspect a good deal, but the time has come for plain speech. They ought to be told, and given permission to go."

"They cannot be ignorant," Theodora said. "They know very well how their Faction regard them. Let them be brought here. You will see that they know what will happen. They ought not to be in the Palace after the setting of the watches." "Bring them," Justinian said. I went out at once, and across the courts to the quarters where they lived. Both men had the privilege of the purple edge, as well as Senatorial rank. Hypatius had lately married a lady of much beauty and goodness. Her name was Mary.

I was shewn to a room where the two brothers were playing chess against her. I am sure that they all expected a summons of the sort, for their cloaks lay ready to hand, and they started with me

at once. We crossed the courts in the glare of the
burning. Smoke and smuts were drifting about; it
was like a walk in hell. When we entered the
Council Room, Phocas explained the situation,
and Justinian said: "You have loyally kept your
promises to myself. This Palace is now a fortress
of the Blue Faction and the Dynasty. We feel that
you should now leave it, and return to your home
outside the Palace precincts." Pompeius, who was
much readier of speech than his brother, said that
they were under obligations of life and death to
Justinian, and would be constant to them. "But
if we go to our homes," he said, "if we leave the
Palace, beyond all doubt some of these rioters will
insist on crowning my brother as Emperor. He
does not want that, any more than I do, but it is
certain to happen. Think, Majesty, to what you
will drive us."

Hypatius said: "You are our Emperor. We prefer to stay by our Emperor when he is in such
danger."

It was said that Hypatius could never open his
mouth without endangering his cause and outrag-
ing his friends. His voice and the words he used
always raised prejudice against him. All present
felt that he had said the very words which were
most certain to make Justinian suspect. Mary,
who had a swift tact to tell her of the situation,
said: "Majesty, might it not be a good thing to

send us to the Asian shore, or down with this wind to Smyrna."

Now this would have been a very good thing, which would have saved much unhappiness if done the day before or the day before that. When she mentioned it, The Count rose from his place and whispered to Justinian. The thought which had come into his mind was that if they went to the Asian shore they would meet troops returning from the war, and might indeed already be in league with them. He was always swift to suspect, he passed his suspicion to Justinian, who had another suspicion, that this might have been suggested to discover what ships might be moving to the Asian shore and how near the troops might be to The City. I knew, as we all knew, that all three, the two brothers and Mary, had vexed the Emperor, we did not know why or how. He hesitated and then said: "The time for that is past. There is certainly an intrigue for the opening of the gates here to take you from the Palace. It is necessary that you leave the Palace at once. The Count will see that you reach your home in safety."

I saw Pompeius make a gesture of despair. Hypatius was vexed and angered; he never could hide his vexation when Justinian gave him orders. Mary, who was the wise one of the three, turned to the Empress and said: "Madam, may I beg you to intercede for us, that we be sent to some House

of Monks of Sanctuary, in Sycæ, across the water.
There we could neither threaten you nor be
threatened." The Empress was touched, but the
request was not one that could be granted. "It
cannot be," she said gently. "There is no sanctuary to these people. Your safety depends on your
going quietly to your home, and refusing what the
mob may wish. If you stay, you will provoke rebellion within these walls. If you go, you may refuse to help rebellion. You can serve us truly by
going."

Mary wept, knowing within herself what might
happen. "Madam, we will go," she said. The
Count opened the door for them. "I'll see you to
your house," he said. Mary bowed to Emperor
and Empress. Pompeius saluted Justinian, bowed
to Theodora and followed Mary. Hypatius seemed
about to say something; he swallowed it down,
saluted, flushed, and went angrily to the door.

The Emperor dismissed the Council then. He
went into his Quarters, with The Empress and
Phocas. I found myself with Procopius, who suggested that I should come to·have supper with him
at his office. He said: "Did you see Ride-A-Cock-
Snort's face as he went out, just then?"

"Who is Ride-A-Cock-Snort?" I asked.

"Why, Hypatius," he said, "did you never hear
the rhyme? It was made when he lost the army up
there in the North.

Ride-A-Cock-Snort,
Didn't like thought,
Only liked sport.
He was licked when he fought;
But before they licked him
Our youth was his victim.

I thought that everybody knew that."

I have no doubt that Procopius had himself made the verses within the last few minutes, upon his first sight of Hypatius. The name Ride-A-Cock-Snort was curiously apt for the creature; he had a queer, bobbing walk, and his nose had been bred away, like the nose of a lap-dog; he could hardly breathe through his nose; his mouth was always open, shewing his front teeth, Yet it was said that when he had lost the army he had only saved himself by wading far out to sea and breathing through his nose.

We went up to the walls after supper. Procopius, who was ribald in his speech at that time, said that The City now looked like a beloved mouth from which the front teeth had been pulled. Indeed, the simile was apt. The fair aspect of the Great Church, beautiful in all weathers, was now gone. It was a shell with holes in it. Smoke drifted from the holes, and gusts of wind made glowings on the walls, so that we could not but mark the ruin made. If you have not looked

on such a sight, you cannot tell what feelings of
misery, defeat, helplessness and rage such things
stir. This had been the soul of The City, and this
defilement of it had been the work of citizens, who
had but begun. Procopius was one used to the dis-
comfort of war, and not knowing how the next
night would be passed, whether in a palace or a
ditch; he said: "If those fellows had any energy,
they would ruin us."

I said: "What do you mean by energy? They
have burned about a fifth of The City."

"That is not energy," he said, "that is just stu-
pidity and bestiality. If those sporting lords had
any brains up above their digestions they would
have made some fires over yonder, and Justinian's
star would set to-morrow." He flung his hand out
towards the East. "They have had all their hundreds of horse; they haven't had the wit to get a
hundred across the water there to burn the ships
Tino has sent to ferry his army by. They claim
hunting as a training for war. Yet not one hunting
man has been better than an imbecile in all the
Persian campaign. And not one in this has shewn
himself any better."

"There is still time," I said, "this campaign is
young yet."

"O anything may happen," he said. "But I feel
one thing to be sure in war, if you don't use your
advantage, you lose it."

I did not like the man, but he had had much strange experience, which made him cynical, and sometimes amusing. He had won his position, of Counsellor to The Eastern Army, by shrewdness and hard work, two qualities which made him judge the idle and the imbecile, whom long custom and the privilege of place had made officers above him. Just before we left the wall that night, he said to me: "It is a race. If those fellows attack the Palace to-morrow morning, as soon as it is light, our throats will all be cut by noon. If they delay their attack till the afternoon, we shall get away at dark by sea, join the Army and make a war of it. If they give us the whole day to-morrow, as they may, since they have given us so much already, then they will not have the ghost of another chance. Good night."

He nodded, and went down the steps; he did not seem to mind the thought of having his throat cut. I did.

When he had gone, I went back to the Reports Room, to meet officers, and to read the latest reports, which had come in by signal-flashes, spies, or messengers. A man was saying: "That fellow Protarchus has come in to Eighth Ward with the best part of a thousand horse. That will about decide matters, I judge."

I said: "Well, horse cannot scale walls." He looked at me with some contempt and said: "They can control the entire life of The City at least."

It was pretty grim in the Reports Room among those young men, each with some good reason for despising the Administration, or, perhaps, for blaming the Administration which had put all their youthful talents in such peril. Some were a little drunk, and one was gloomily saying: "I shall be killed to-morrow; I know it." I went again into the court-yards, to walk about in the cold, in the stink of burning, in the presence of that destruction, hearing the cat-calls from outside. "Dirty Usurping Dogs. Your throats'll all be cut to-morrow. Conquer, Conquer."

After this, I lay down for a little, not to sleep, but to ponder on Protarchus' coming, and on possible ways of turning this to our advantage. I saw a scheme, and shrank from it, then returned to it, and at last felt that it ought to be tried.

On this I went straight to Justinian. I had expected to find him abed, but he was standing at his plain wooden desk reading a law-book by the light of two candles. He had a way of dropping whatever he was doing and giving his whole attention instantly to any officer who came to him on service. This is a rare faculty, and a part of his greatness. "Ha, Origen," he said, "you have some subtle device, I see."

"It is for you to say if it be not a foolish device, Majesty," I said. "Protarchus must be against these anarchists. Why should we not get the priests to urge Protarchus against Bessus?"

"I do not think that Protarchus needs urging," he said. "How will that help us?"

"It will make a division among your enemies."

"The division is there already," he said, "but it can hardly become acute."

"Lord," I said, "let me try to make it acute. Let me stir up the trouble, by saying, that Pompeius and Hypatius have been put out of the Palace. They can hardly know that yet. They cannot know it. Directly they hear it, half The City will rally to them. The City is sick and terrified of disorder. They'll rally round the two; they will flock to Protarchus, and beg him to end the disorder by fighting Bessus and the gangs and crowning Hypatius, in a Civic Election, as Emperor."

"I thought that I was Emperor," he said.

"Majesty," I said, "God forbid that I should ever think otherwise. But I see this as a desperate expedient to stop an attack upon this Palace tomorrow morning. If there be no diversion, this will be attacked."

"Yes," he said. "Whatever wins time, wins war. But let me tell you this: the movement you speak of has already begun. The Sixth Ward clergy are already with Protarchus, urging something of the kind. But you know, Origen, that Protarchus and his kind rather want Bessus and his men to have

the task of killing me; it will put me out of the
way, and all the blood-guilt on Bessus. I am in-
clined to think that the Palace will be attacked
early to-morrow."

"Lord," I said, "I believe that this Hypatius
business might be made to delay it, if you would
give me leave to try. And, Lord, in the meantime,
disarm the Palace garrison; let the Count's Barbarians be the only garrison till the Army be
here."

"That has already been arranged," he said. He
looked at me with his charming smile and clapped
me on the shoulder. "And so this young man from
Argos thinks he might delay disaster. Do you
know, I believe you have a kind of instinct which
is what the world calls genius."

"Lord," I said, "I know that you have the genius which is the only thing I wish to call Master.
You and the Lady, your Empress."

He looked at me fixedly; he said nothing, but I
knew that he was pleased.

"Lord," I said, "will you tell me what you were
reading when I came in?"

"Look," he said.

I went to his desk and took up the parchment.
It was an old roll of Law. Synesius' Comments on
Recent Additions to the Laws of Land Convey-
ance, as they affect Municipal Properties.

"With so much Municipal Property destroyed,"

he said, "it is important to know how we stand. Now, look, Origen, sleep in the Palace; but leave it before it is light. The face of the rebellion is changing all the time; it may have profoundly changed before morning; all sorts of sub-plots are seething and bubbling up and it may be a different thing to-morrow. Two things are sure to happen. Hypatius will be crowned, and we shall be attacked. If words from you can delay either matter even an hour, it may make a difference." He shook my hand; and I withdrew, feeling sure that I should never see him again. He was getting me out of the Palace before destruction fell. He had perhaps some little lingering hope, that some of his Army might still be in time; he saw that I saw this or thought this, for as I reached the door, he said: "The point about miracles is, that they are not repeated." He referred to a time just before his crowning, when he had been threatened by a plot; then, the return of troops to The City just in time had saved his Dynasty; he could hardly expect such Fortune twice.

I had an hour or two of uneasy sleep, waking often, to what I thought were the rabble entering. When I could endure bed no longer, I went up the wall-top, where I found The City quiet in the cold, but looking like a suburb of Hell, from the occasional glare of burning ruin; no other lights shewed. A monastery far off rang for a service. It was the one monastery which the mob had spared, being the one which had rescued the three from execution; all the rest had been pillaged and shut up. I asked a soldier, a subaltern of the Barbarians, what had happened in the night. He said: "It is as you see, quiet. But something is happening yonder."

He pointed away towards the distant Eighth Ward where now and again lights passed from west to east across a space bare of building. At that distance, I could not say if they were men or carts with lanterns. I asked if word had come in what these lights were.

"Yes," he said, "the crowd is setting towards Fifth Ward. It may have to do with the man Hypatius."

I remembered then what Procopius had said, about a possible attack on ships sent by the Emperor to ferry his Army when it drew near. I said to myself, that I would slip down to the Waterfront, to speak with the naval officers there and find out if these people with the lights going eastward were Green horse riding forth to destroy those ships.

When I reached the Waterfront, the eastern sky was all bright with morning; the lanterns whatever they had been, were no longer to be seen. The Naval Officers said that no troops with or without lights had been passing round the Harbour during the night, and that I could see for myself how impossible it would be for horsemen to cross the Bosphorus while patrol-boats were in the channel there. To convince me, he took me into his despatch-boat, ran up the sail, and glided swiftly out into the sea, till the channel opened. We stood up channel a little; his men signalled to the guard-boats and the signal stations, and had answers from them. "You see?" my officer said, "they cannot get across without shipping, nor unobserved. Hullo, though, what is that?"

Rather far up the channel, coming down towards us with the current and the brisk cold wind, were two big, black, north-country ships. "North-countrymen, sir," one of our boat-hands said. The waiting guard-boats dashed out upon these, signalling to them to stop for examination; and they did stop, in a measure, going up into the wind, and putting over their delayers. "They come from beyond Trebizond," my officer said. "They usually lay up for the winter-months; but sometimes they make a dash for it, when the weather seems settled; and if they get through, of course they reap a profit from it. Of course, sometimes they don't get through. Well; we'll turn back; there's nothing doing here."

Those two ships were to have a great influence upon our fortunes, little as I thought it at that moment.

It was strangely cheering to talk with this young officer, to whom the problem of the Dynasty was so simple. To him the rebels were simply "those fellows" who would soon be knocked back into order; they were just ill-birds, who fouled their nest, The City. His own task was simple, and thoroughly done; the rebels were not to use the Harbour nor the sea. While he lived, I knew that that part of Justinian's Empire was safe. When I landed, I knew that the rest of it had passed into rebel hands.

It was easy to feel the change in people as I moved among them inland to the heart of the Fifth Ward. During the night, they had come to feel that Justinian was finished with; he had had his chance, and had failed to preserve the very heart and crown of his City; since he could not keep his City, let others have it who could; the change was profound. The night before, probably, all would have said: "We will endure anything rather than submit to creatures like Bessus and Rufinus"; now, the word had come that Protarchus offered them an alternative, and the tide of The City was flowing that way at once. I went with it, to that part of the Fifth Ward where certain very old families had their very old family mansions. I flowed with the tide to the back of the mansion, known as the Anastasian Home, which had given a Patriarch, three Consuls and an Emperor to our

State. I went along the side of this house to the main road in front of it; I could get no further because of the crowd, which filled that road, manned the railings beyond it, and the grassy square beyond the railings. Somewhere in the crowd a band was playing a Dinner-Green march. I asked a man: "What is happening?" He looked at me with some contempt for not already knowing, and said: "We're changing Emperors; making Hypatius Emperor." At that moment the crowd in front of the house began to wave caps and shout. I could not see it, but I knew from this that Hypatius must have appeared upon a balcony. I should have thought that the appearance of Hypatius, as well as his appalling public record of incompetence and disaster, would have sufficed to damn him in the eyes of any citizen, but no; here were these hundreds of men shouting "Hypatius. Good old Hypatius. The good old Green forever." My neighbour turned to me again and said: "That's what we want in an Emperor, a gent and a sportsman; not any of your scholars what knows nothing but law-books."

"Can you see him?" I asked.

"No. I can't see him," he said. "But I know him all right; he's got Blood. He's got what can't be pretended-to."

It is strange, but one of the points most frequently urged against Justinian in those days was,

that he was intelligent; another was, that he sprang
from a family which had nothing but its own energy. It is incredible to what depths of fatuity the
citizens sank at the suggestions of a few astute
scoundrels and the keepers-on of blinkers. No
doubt, I should have heard about the virtues of
Blood as exemplified in Ride-A-Cock-Snort, had
not one of the great Green orators, stationed at
the railing just opposite Hypatius, begun at that
instant to speak. I caught a glimpse of the speaker
by craning my neck; he seemed to be mostly
mouth; with rags of black hair around it. He was
Theagenes the Patriot, a very well-known orator,
with a marvellous voice and a familiarity which
made him adored throughout the City; he was
called Thajji, Good old Thajji.

"My great Lord Hypatius," he cried, "we here
are the Sovereign People. We here are your People. We are the Will of your People. We come
here with a prayer to you: Which we hope you
will grant: Which we know you will grant. On
your granting it depends our happiness, Depends
our Future, Depends our Liberty." The people at
that time always shouted at the word Liberty;
they usually do; though God knows they seldom
know what they mean by it. They cheered now, as
though it meant everything. Thajji was visibly
blown up by the cheering; it is the orator's motive
force. "My great Lord Hypatius," he went on,

"we, here, the Sovereign People in lawful community assembled. By virtue of our Sovereign Right. By virtue of the Empire's need. By virtue of your most rightful claim now fully acknowledged . . ." (Here one of the crowd leaders rapped at the man near him, "Cheer, you bastards; cheer".) When the cheers died down into a silence Thajji made his point. "We declare you the lawful Emperor." There was a storm of cheering. He then called for "Three cheers for the Emperor Hypatius", then for three cheers more; then for others. Then in the midst of the roaring and shouting, the band played

> "Green, 'tis the fair land's garment,
> I therefore hold it dear"

and everybody yelled as though the silly words meant something, and as though the colour meant a principle. I could not see anything to which all the tumult was addressed; but when there came a lull, I could hear a voice, a woman's voice, trying to make itself heard in that direction. "It's his wife," my neighbour said. "It's his wife or something; overcome or something." Some of the men in front of the house were laughing and others mocking. Thajji and others shouted: "No, Madam, none can refuse the Sovereign People. He is our Emperor and The Beautiful Good Mary is our

Empress. Boys, you see your Empress. God save our Empress Mary. Three cheers for our lovely Empress."

The crowd cheered, and cheered, so that for some minutes it was impossible to hear anything said by any of the leaders. It occurred to me (though I could see very little) that the great City families, and western lords, were not present at this gathering. They had no doubt paid for it; and contrived to set it going; Thajji and his men were their paid tools; but I had no doubt that the intention was to make this offer of the Empire appear to be a popular matter, springing from the wish of the citizens who were both shocked at the excesses of the extremists and the apathy of the Ruling Dynasty. Thajji no doubt enjoyed the meeting hugely; he had a peculiar, terrible genius for things of the kind. His instinct bade him hurry; a mob must be kept active. He was not going to let his lovely Empress delay matters. He made his band play a flourish; then he shouted: "Boys. Only one thing remains. We must take our Emperor to the old Market of our ancestors. We must crown him as Constantine was crowned. By the People. For the People. In the People's Market. Come on, boys. Our Emperor to the Market."

He had fifty men to do his bidding; the real race-course bodyguard of boxers and bashers.

These men, putting their heads down, thrust a way to the mansion door; they not only made the way, they kept it, when made. The band drew nearer and struck up the Emperor's March; the crowd yelled applause. I saw Thajji and two other leaders, one of them was the Archon of Fourth Ward, an embalmer of bodies by trade, go forward to welcome Hypatius down. Now Mary, who was a noble spirit, knew well that her man was not fitted for rule, and that his could only lead to disaster. She is said to have flung herself at her husband's feet, imploring him not to go. I squirmed my way past my neighbours at this point, and though they cursed me, and struck at me, they did not do more than hurt somebody else. I wriggled towards the mansion, till I reached a point just behind the bodyguard. I saw Thajji and the embalmer (a man with an appalling face of callous, cynical calculation) enter the mansion. I could not have believed that such a thing could have happened, but they went straight to Hypatius, seized him, dragged him again to the balcony and called out. "Our new Emperor shews himself to his People." The crowd cheered and shrieked: "Bring him to the Market. Crown him. Crown him. Hypatius. The Emperor Hypatius."

"We are leading him to the Market," Thajji called; and at that they started to lead him; they had him between them, so that he could not get away, though he struggled a little, not liking the handling of an embalmer and a cheap orator. In a minute they had him out of the door, pulling him, as I saw, from the hands of his wife, who was in frantic tears, beseeching them to let him go, praying to him not to leave Mary, and crying: "It is death; it can only lead to death." The band was already off towards the Market, playing the Emperor's March. The race-course bashers pulled Mary from her husband. "Come, lady," they said, "will you come along to see your Husband crowned? He's only going to be made Emperor. You don't want to be alarmed." She struggled to rejoin her husband, but this they were not going to allow. "No, if you won't come quietly, you'll just go back, Madam," and at this about a dozen of them bundled her back into her house. She had no further chance of coming near to her man, for the crowd had swept in after the marchers, and I was swept with it, all of us singing the Emperor's Pæan and cheering for Hypatius. In very good order, with songs and shoutings we soon drew out of that quarter to what had been The City's chief Market, the lovely open space of Constantine.

Alas, it was now filthy from the burnings and tramplings, all the gaiety and plenty were gone. There were black ruins across all one side; on the north were all the mess, huttery and camp-fires of Bessus' camps. The stone throne or rostrum where the auctioneers had sold big shiploads of stuff, still stood of course. They helped Hypatius up this, and again shewed him to the people. Bessus' soldiers were forming up on their side of the space; they hardly took any notice of these doings.

It was clear to me, that they were not well-pleased at all by this crowning business, and held very different views of what The City needed. What part they might play later was doubtful. I watched their sullen bearing as they slowly formed up, and judged, that these crowners might have trouble from them. But now the play developed round the auctioneer's rostrum.

I had from the first noticed a party of men not far from the rostrum. They had all been standing quietly, each man wrapped in a cloak of dull green with yellow trimmings. I had at first taken them for a gang of savages, from some tribe beyond the Danube. As Hypatius went up the steps, these men turned to him and flung back their cloaks, with a concerted gesture. I saw then that they were Senators and Most Expensives of the Quadriga (racing and political) Club. They were the Dinner-Green lords, the pillars of the Hippodrome, to most of whom a charioteer who could wreck an enemy's team without fouling it was the noblest work of God. Their tough and brainless faces seemed now almost alive, as they waddled forward on their bandy legs, half of them chewing

straws like ostlers, and each taking pride in having
very old Club coats. The admission to The Quadriga was difficult; there was always a pride in
shewing ancient membership by wearing the Club
cloak till it fell to pieces. Among the party, though
of course not wearing Club cloaks, were some of
the hard-mouthed rather drunken women of that
set. One of them I recognised as a notorious creature who had tried on one occasion to drive a
team in the Hippodrome, but the charioteers had
ducked her in the horse-troughs and turned her
out. This party now advanced to below the rostrum. One of the Lords went up the steps to him
and shouted aloud: "Lord Hypatius. Elect of The
People. The Senate and People here assembled
now summon you to assume the Throne."

I was not far from the rostrum; I am sure that
Hypatius said nothing of any kind in answer to
the summons. His face was an odd mixture of
terror, loathing, and gratified vanity. I could read
on his strange fatal face relief at meeting members
of The Quadriga Club after his half-hour with
the embalmer; but he was unable to speak; he
cleared his throat once or twice. The Lord who
had addressed him was one who had been a pugi-
list when young: he had a cauliflower ear of which
he was vain, for in the fashion of his set, he called
attention to it by wearing a large turquoise ear-
ring in it. This man, with his foxy, battered face,

and the slow movements of one who has moved too fast in youth and now has an engorged heart, winked at one of his followers, and said to one of the hard-mouthed women beside him: "Give us your necklace, C'rinna, I've got to crown this prize-entry." I was by this time beside him, and can vouch for the words. The woman, Corinna, said: "I'm not going to give it. I'll lend it, as long as I get it back again."

"Come on," he said, "you'll get it back this afternoon, and be made Lady of his Bed-Chamber for the loan of it."

At this, Corinna smiled, and took off the necklace, which was a gold chain, interspersed with gold beads. She said: "You'll never make it a crown. I must shorten it." She quickly hooked the clip into one of the links, so that it made a smaller round. The old fighter took it and shouted aloud: "People of Byzantium. Is it your Will that I now crown your new Emperor?" The crowd shouted that it was. One of the Senators said: "Be sure you say 'Senate and People'."

The foxy one shouted: "In the name of the Senate and the People here lawfully assembled, I now crown thee the Emperor Hypatius. Long live the Emperor Hypatius."

He put the necklace on Hypatius' head, as the crowd shouted Long live the Emperor Hypatius. God bless our Emperor, and so forth. The lady had made the ring of gold too small. It just sat, as a gold ring on the top of Hypatius' skull, with an end of gold dangling down and getting into his eye. It balanced uneasily on his skull; he had to put up his hand to keep it there. He looked such a figure of fun that one could not but be sorry for him and sorrier for the poor woman to whom this creature was all the world. One of the Senators near me, an active, witty and unpleasant man, who had been much enriched by Army contracts under the Emperor Anastasius, said: "We must hide this creature before he's a mock." He leaped up to the rostrum, and shouted: "People of Byzantium. We have taken the first step to save our City. We have crowned our Emperor. Now for the next step to save the City. The Senate must enter secret conclave with the Emperor. And you, People of Byzantium, await your Emperor's order."

While the people shouted, this Senator said: "Quick, your Majesty. The Senate must meet under the colonnade there. Come down with me, quickly. Follow on, Most Illustrious."

There was one colonnade not destroyed by the fire; this gave shelter from the wind and a partial privacy. He hustled the Emperor into this shelter; I followed with some of the Senators. I heard him say to Hypatius: "Don't take off your crown, whatever you do. That would be an omen. Now,

Most Illustrious, you are Emperor. You must decide the next step."

Hypatius said: "People of the Senate, Most Illustrious, before we begin our deliberations, it would be a good thing, I mean it is customary to obtain the blessing of the Patriarch."

"No, no, no, Majesty," the Senators cried, half a dozen together, "the Senate and People suffice; the sacring can follow. This is war; we must decide what is next to be done."

The confusion among them made the new Ruler still more confused; and at this point, the ranks of Bessus marched up. Bessus entered, into the shelter of the colonnade, followed by the elegant little Rufinus, both men walking with a certainty and insolence which made those patricians white with rage. Rufinus took the word at once. He said: "Emperor and Senate, we, the People, declare that this is no time for delay or debate, but for action against the public enemy. We, the People, demand that you lead us at once against the Usurper in the Palace."

You will recollect that the mob was seething round the outskirts of the colonnade, pressing on the very skirts of the Senators. Rufinus and Bessus had found a place at the side, upon some unburned bales. They had a dozen spearmen with them, and these men took the cue and shouted:

"Come on to the Palace, you patrician bastards, don't dally here. Cut Justinian's throat. To the Palace. Attack the Palace." The men of Bessus' army shouted: "Attack the Palace. Come on, Emperor, draw your sword and let's be doing. We're going to attack the Palace."

The Senators who had just crowned Hypatius were all somewhat staggered by this; they were not very ready; they looked to Hypatius for a lead; he, of course, gave them none. What they wanted was order in the City, not more licence from an armed mob not in their control. Bessus and Rufinus were as deadly enemies to them as Justinian. It was a chance for me; my task was to delay any attack upon the Palace. A sort of spiritual hand seemed to grip my soul and thrust me forward, saying: "Now's the time."

So with a shout of: "Emperor, Senators, August People of Byzantium, listen to Origen from Argos," I was on the bale, towering up above Rufinus, and holding all the attention. The words seemed to flow of themselves, and from the first second I held them; they were hot wax to the moulder. "Friends," I shouted. "We have declared war on the Usurper. We shall make war on the Usurper. War will end the Usurper. But not war upon the Palace, where he has all the advantage of fortress walls, and trained troops and inexhaustible supplies. We can end the Usurper much more easily.

We can show him that he is no longer Emperor. What if he live in the Palace of the Emperors? Are there no other Palaces? There is Placinian Palace; and Helen's Palace; both Royal Courts for a new Dynasty. I say, let our new Emperor take up residence in one of those; let all come there to kiss hands; let the Patriarch come to offer sacring. The Usurper will know at once that he is no longer Emperor; he will fly; no need for the People to attack him. Let the police take him as he runs. Friends, Senators, August Emperor of the People, do not go to attack the Palace. Go to the Hippodrome. Take the Emperor's seat in the Royal Box. Appoint this great soldier . . ." here I shewed Bessus: "Your new Commander-in-Chief . . . and this wise statesman . . ." here I shewed Rufinus: "Your præfect. Appoint from this gathering of your nobility your Ambassadors, your Household, your Judges and your Provincial Præfects. But first to the Hippodrome; assume the Purple. Ascend the throne and be in deed and truth our Emperor Hypatius. Friends. Lead our Emperor to the Hippodrome."

It is said, that the orator's power over men is not one that a wise man should covet, and that pride in such power is a deadly danger. Power can be misused; no doubt I misused it then; I misled that mob, wilfully, being at war with it and with its leaders. I suppose that no one can

exert power of any sort without an exaltation. I
felt an exaltation as I spoke, and knew that I had
swayed my hearers, yet I knew, too, that the words
came into my mind from some well that was not
under my direction. What spirit it was which
prompted me to bring in Bessus and Rufinus I
cannot imagine; it was no conscious thought of
mine. Yet without that happy thought the fate of
The City might have been so different. As I finished with my cry "To the Hippodrome", all that
mad fluid, the mob, with its dam-gates lifted,
found a direction. Instantly, it broke into the
direction with a yell: "To the Hippodrome." All
the leaders at once surged off as the spirit bade.
There was cheering; the bands struck up the Imperial March. From my bale-top, I could see that
the outer fringes of the mob had somehow learned
what had been said at the heart. Hypatius had no
power to withstand the impulse even if he had
wished it. He probably thought at the moment
what all about him thought, that he was Emperor,
really Emperor, and that at the Hippodrome, he
would sit in the Emperor's throne, and appoint
his officers over distant provinces and subject
races. The instant may have been strangely beautiful and exalted to him. He smiled and said:
"Lead on to the Hippodrome, my People." The
shrewd and sinister face of Bessus had lit up with
a smile at my unexpected mention of him; he gave

me a swift nod of recognition. The dapper face of Rufinus gleamed, too; he tapped his chin, which was a way he had when pleased. They knew how to profit from the instant; they had their tasks at once made clear to them; they went to their parties.

Now, to the blaring bands, the flood set off to the Hippodrome; banners appeared from somewhere; it was a fine sight to see them swing into order to the music and pass on their way. I let them go. I was shaken by what I had done, and sat on the bale to recover myself; when I was a little restored, I took off my sandals and put them on again, tying the thongs with hands which shook. After that, I rose up and left the market, which was now deserted save by some of the camp cooks of Bessus' men, who were cutting up a stolen sheep for the mid-day meal. As soon as I was out of their sight, I went back to the Palace postern on the Waterfront, and was there admitted. It was necessary to pretend not to be in any hurry, until I was safely inside the walls; then, I ran as fast as I could to the Quarters, to find Justinian.

At the door of the Quarters, two or three young officers were talking. In those times of stress, one knew by instinct what side the next person favoured; I knew that those men were Hypatians, and that the Dynasty had received bad news since daylight; the crowning of Hypatius was bad enough; but I knew that something worse had happened; and that these little traitors were hugging it to their dirty little bosoms. I was not going to ask them what it was. They tried to stop me from going in. They said that the Emperor was with the Court at a very important Council; however, they were not going to stop me; I pushed on to the ante-room, usually guarded by Justinian's own clansmen, but now held by three old Senators from Justinian's part of the world. One of them knew me; he looked about as cheerful as a mourner at a tomb, but opened the door to let me through. I went in, to the big room facing on the sea.

The Council had been going on, round the table for half an hour or more; it had now broken up, and all were on their feet. The Emperor and Empress were near the great window looking on the sea; the Count, Belisarius, was saying: "It's unfortunate, of course."

I asked Phocas under my breath: "What is unfortunate?"

He whispered: "The Army won't be here to-day; there's snow in Happy Valley." Justinian turned to me with his smile. "Here is Origen, who always brings good news; what new joy have you to tell us, Origen?"

I did not feel that it was much joy, but I told it; after all, there was some delay in the attack

upon us. Justinian said: "Did I not tell you, Origen always brings good news? Now, what is to
keep us from an attack on these rebels in the Hippodrome?"

Old Symmachus said: "I hardly think they will
stay long in the Hippodrome in this cold wind."

"They will, Lord," I said. "They will be there
all morning, for people coming in will keep others
from getting away."

Justinian gave me a charming look. "Come,
now," he said. "I have not called on our Palace
garrison to do anything since this trouble began.
But now I am for calling on them."

Phocas said: "Don't try it, Majesty. You can't
depend on them."

"I have not tried them yet," Justinian answered.
"Soldiers will always respond, if the matter is put
to them in the right way. I believe that they
would follow me, if I went down and asked them
to come out with me."

Basilides shook his head, and said: "No, no,
Majesty; indeed, it is not so; they would not."

The Count said: "They say I only care for Bar-
barian soldiers; it isn't so; the men of this City
are the best troops in the world. But the Præfect
tells you the truth about the gang in your present
garrison. I've no trust in those fellows. They don't
like fighting and they don't like you; they are just
waiting to see what will happen."

"Very good," Justinian said, "I will be the thing that will happen. I'll go down and call them out."

"Majesty," the Count said. "You'd provoke immediate mutiny; they won't go."

"That is true, Sire," Phocas said.

John of Cappadocia, who sat there sullen and bloodshot, but resolute and ready as always when things were black, said: "The thing to do is to sit tight where you are, Sire. Those dogs, the garrison, may not like you, but they like their own throats, and they know that those aren't safe from those friends of Liberty outside the walls yonder. They've got sense enough to resist, if those fellows attack."

"Sir," Phocas said. "My enquiries lead to the very opposite opinion. If we are attacked our garrison mean to open the gates."

"They can't open the gates," John answered. "The Count's bodyguard is holding the gates and the walls."

"Thank you for your good opinion of my bodyguard," the Count said, "but it works out at one man to every ten yards of wall. That's how your gates and walls are held at present."

"There are ourselves," John growled. "And the Palace servants, and the Customs and Water-Guard men. The Army MUST be here in three days;

may be here in two. I say, we can hold this Palace
till the Army's here."

"Sir," the Count said, "that's the spirit; a fighting spirit, and that's the spirit I respect; but
though I'm a soldier, I've got some sense. I say
that any resolute commander with the forces those
dogs have got could take this Palace in half an
hour. What's to stop them? They've five thousand men; we've got a doubtful five hundred, and
a couple of hundred others ready to stab us in
the back and open the gates."

Procopius had been warned, I think, to take
this as his cue. He said: "Majesty, as a War-
Councillor, I have to advise prudence. The pru-
dent course for you and for the most noble
Lady our Empress, is to go to your advancing
Army. You would be safe with them to-morrow.
I don't think there can be any question of that.
If the fair weather hold, as seems likely, you will
be back here with them the day after. There can
be no doubt whatever, that the riot will collapse
directly the Army appears here."

"That is my opinion as a soldier, Majesty," the
Count said, "that you should fall back on to your
supports. There is no disgrace in falling back on
your supports; it is often wise soldiership."

The Naval Officer for the Month said: "The
Treasurer ordered me to embark the Private Chest

at dawn this morning. It is on board, under my guard there, with shipping-space for at least fifty people, if you decide to go to your Army, Majesty. I think that you would be with your Advanced Guards by dawn to-morrow, and perhaps back in the City to-morrow night."

"Having fled from it?" Justinian said.

"No, Lord," the Count said. "It is not a question of flying. It is a question of saving your Cause; and as a soldier, I say that that is the answer."

The Empress had been silent all this time. She had stood, not far from her husband, as it were framed in the light of the great window. She was not tall, and there was never anything in her face or person which man could call beautiful exceedingly; yet most men have agreed, that when she was in a room they could look at no other woman. She never used any of the vulgarities of fashion which the wives of the Illustrious practised. She never had her eyebrows plucked, nor painted her finger-nails blue, green or any other colour. She used no paint upon her face, and never bedevilled her hair. All men are agreed that she was the one woman of The City who looked well-dressed when the Persian, Indian or Ethiopian women were in the Court. She took great pains with her appearance. She daily did those practices and exercises prescribed for the Imperial Ballet. These exercises gave her the grace for which she was at all times famous. Her walk was superb. She was fond of subtle and very beautiful colours and of fine stuffs. She spent much time in the Imperial silk-rooms, supervising the dyeings and weavings. She had a genius for costume; she designed her own, and often caused skeins to be dyed to a tint she wished. She was at that moment wearing a dark winter dress designed to shew off a remarkable blue which she had caused to be struck. It was an unusual and singularly lovely colour; the silk caught the light; and I remember watching her with amazement as she stood near the window, with this exquisite colour on her, and thinking, as her shrewd eyes turned from face to face, that she was like an unearthly bird. Her friend, the great dancer, Macedonia, gave always something of the same impression, with this difference, that you expected nothing save lovely movement from Macedonia, but from the Empress you expected wisdom. She had not spoken until this instant; now she spoke to the Count. "Is it an answer, Count?" she said. "Is it not a putting off of an answer?" There was some rudeness always in the Count; he came from a rough school and disliked the intrusion of women in affairs. At that time, he hardly knew the Empress; and possibly thought that she was one of the insolent patrician women who meddled with politics and gave away State secrets. At any rate, he replied now, hotly: "It is a soldier's answer, Madam. I don't know when women began to meddle with soldiering, nor why."

"I do not know when, nor why," she said. "This is not a time to discuss whether women should speak their minds when men are weakening. In a great danger one must be wise and swift. I say that this is not a time for flight, even if it save life. No man who has come into the light can avoid Death; but no man who has come into Kingship can bear the shame of being a runaway. May I never be parted from this Sea-Blue" (she touched the silk on her shoulder) "nor live on that day when those happening on me shall not call me Queen." She turned towards Justinian with an indescribable exquisite sweetness and tenderness, which, indeed, she always shewed to him, and went on: "If it be your wisdom to save yourself, O King, nothing checks it. We have much wealth, yonder is the sea; there are the ships. But consider whether, later, you may not think that Death would have been sweeter than safety. For myself, I prize an old saying 'Queenship is a beautiful shroud'."

Justinian had been looking at her; indeed, no one there could have taken his eyes from her. Justinian smiled and gave her a little nod. They understood each other, those two.

"By God, Madam," the Count said, "you are a real soldier."

Not one of those present but felt that she had cleared the sky; we would all rather have died, than leave. Then, at that very moment of lightening, the sun shone in at the window from a cloud, and there came the piped call for a Naval Captain entering the Quarters.

Justinian seemed puzzled, for he knew of no Sea-Commander about to return to report. Almost at once, the door was tapped and one of the old Senators announced that the Commander Moundos wished for leave to report himself, from the Euxine.

"Let him enter," Justinian said. "It is Moundos, who has been away in Tauris breaking up the pirates there."

Moundos appeared a moment later, knelt to Justinian, then rose, saluted, knelt to the Empress and kissed her hand; then rose again, stood back, saluted, and waited for the Emperor's commands. He was a young man, with a face of much resolution all tanned and beaten by the weather.

"You've been preying upon pirates," Justinian said. "Things have left us rather a prey to pirates here. What men have you with you?"

"I have three companies of Erulians," he said. "The fourth company should be here to-morrow; the fifth will be some days later."

"Three companies?" the Count cried. "You

mean you have brought two hundred and fifty men?"

"Rather more, Sir; three hundred and seven."

"Fit and well; and with weapons?"

"They are paraded now, Sir, with weapons. They hoped the Emperor might be pleased to see them."

"Pleased?" Justinian said. "Never more pleased."

"Tell your men, Sir, to stand easy for a few minutes," the Count said. "Have they had any food?"

"Yes, Sir; they fed before leaving the ship."

As soon as Moundos had gone to set his men at ease, The Count said: "This alters the face of the war. Now we have four hundred and fifty good spearmen, as well as the doubtful garrison. The doubters may think fit to join us now. In any case, we must go up against those fellows in the Hippodrome."

"Who is to guard the Palace gates and walls meanwhile?" John asked. "The doubters?"

"Let the Palace gates and walls sweat," the Count answered coarsely. "In any case you've got a Lady in the garrison here who's a better soldier than any of those dogs in your precious War Department. By God, Madam, I'm proud to serve you."

"What do you intend, Count?" Justinian asked.

"Intend? Why, fight them. This fellow Moundos with his fellows will go round the Hippodrome and come in at the back of the crowd. I shall go with my spearmen straight into the Royal Box by your private entry from the Palace here; and I think your doubting garrison will come with me."

He seemed to look for nothing more than a nod from the Emperor. After all, he knew the ground and had a plan that suited; the Emperor said: "Do it."

I must now try to describe the battlefield.

The Hippodrome is an immense, long, beautiful track for the chariot-racing which was, at that time, the only occupation of the nobility and the main delight of the mob. It is near the Palace. The Imperial Box was entered from the Palace by a passage through a guard-house, where a quarter company of guards was barracked. The Imperial Box was almost a Palace in itself, having in it every space and luxury for the entertainment of the Emperor's guests, and (as people said) the pleasure of the Master of the Horse, who ran the place pretty much for his own delight. The front of the Imperial Box opened upon the Race Course at the column of the winners. Not less than three hundred people could sit in comfort there to watch the racing. Not less than that number, of Dinner-Green Lords, Senators, and the supporters of Bessus, sat there at that time about Hypatius and his brother, who were holding their first

Court, and swearing-in their officers. The Count meant to go through the Guard-House directly upon this party and seize Hypatius where he sat.

The Race Course stretches away from the Imperial Box in an immense expanse. All down the centre of the track are barriers, with columns and works of art; all round its sides are the tiers of seats. On that evil day most of the side nearer to the Palace was burnt out; the seats and buildings had been ruined by the fires; they were a mess of tumbled ruin and rubble, with the blackened teeth of walls sticking up and pockets of fire still smouldering. However this ruin and the cold weather had not kept the citizens away; they had poured into the Hippodrome by every entry, so that all the course and seats and ruins were crowded, and more came flooding in behind them, all pressing-up to see the new Emperor, the wonder of his time, still crowned with the Corinna necklet which would not stay on.

Moundos was to come in behind this crowd, press it up a little tighter, and make it impossible for any rebel troops to interfere with the Count while he seized Hypatius. That was the simple plan. If it had succeeded, it might have ended the rebellion with very little loss of life.

On the order, Moundos led his men out of the Palace by the Snail Gate and at once found himself among the ruins. His men began to clamber and stumble over these, on their way towards the Hippodrome; a more difficult march was never made by men. When they were fairly started the Count marched swiftly and directly towards the Guard-House of the Imperial Box.

The way to this was by a passage from the Palace; he had expected to pass through without any opposition or trouble; but when he was near the Imperial Box, so near, that I, who was with him, could hear the cheers of the lords sitting near Hypatius, he found that the guards inside the Guard-House had dropped the heavy iron grating which barred the passage whenever the Emperor was in the Box. Two sentries were on duty beyond this grating. The Count ordered them to hoist it up and let him through.

The soldiers who were of the Palace garrison, determined to do nothing whatever for Justinian till the situation was clearer, just stared at The Count and pretended not to hear. The Count repeated the order, with the emphasis of a Commander on a very urgent and dangerous mission; the soldiers sniggered, and moved away out of sight. The Count beat and swore; no one took the least notice of him. He was not one to lose time. He turned to me, and said: "About turn; we must try something else. Back there; into the Palace." We turned back.

As we came out of the passage into the court,

we met the Emperor and his two nephews. The Count called to the Emperor, with the grin which he always wore when things were not going well. "It's not our day, Majesty. Your soldiers won't let us through."

"Right," Justinian said, "you will have to go round, then."

"It's bad," The Count said, "I've lost good time." He turned to me, and said: "Just go to Moundos, there, from me, will you, and tell him to mark time, till he sees me in position? You understand, I've got to get my men right round. He must wait for me."

"I understand, Count," I said. The Count said: "I'll try another dodge, too."

As I turned to join Moundos, I heard Justinian say: "My two nephews want to come with you, Count."

"Let all men of good will come with me, Majesty," The Count said. "Now, come on, sons; the sooner, the quicker."

I had had little idea of the ruin caused by the fire till I began to clamber across the mess to Moundos. He had been halted, under cover of some walls, waiting for a signal. I gave the Count's orders, and said that he would have to wait for some time. "I thought so," Moundos said. "Lie down, there, men, except one man from each mess." The men lay down as they could among

the ruins. It had been a street there till Liberty
reached it; now, no roof was left in all its extent.
Moundos took me with him to what had been a
back-window in a rather high-standing house.
There were wisps of smoke still rising from the
ruin on the floor, which gave out a warmth for
which I was glad, for the day, though bright, was
very cold. From the window, I could see all the
long, blackened ruin of that side of the Hippodrome. The seats on that side had been of a
shoddy, makeshift wooden construction, which
had mostly burned, leaving a few stone partitions,
and a few terms, with statues on them. I could see
right into the stadium which was seething full of
people all pressing up towards the Box at the end.
The space in the middle course (being good ma-
sonry) was not burned. It too was crowded with
people; they were clambering up everywhere, to
points from which they could see. They were very
near to us, of course, but not one in a thousand
of them ever turned in our direction; nor would
they have seen us, if they had turned, for our men
snuggled down into shelter and began to play at
dice or that other favourite game of theirs called
Hop-ponk, done with flat bits of bone. The cap-
tains of the messes alone watched the Hippodrome
from cover like ours.

.We waited what seemed like a weary time, seeing nothing of The Count or his men, and won-

dering what was keeping them. Our orders were,
to do nothing till we saw him in position. Our
men were well-content to wait; but Moundos
wished to be attacking, while the chance was ours.

"There is all that dish, just waiting to be
carved," he said. "Are we to wait all day?"

No one answered him; there was no sign of the
Count nor of his Barbarians with their bright hel-
mets. We could see the little tiny hands clapping
in the Imperial Box, as one or other statesman
said some silly thing; we heard the answering
brays of the mob. It was impossible for us to think
that that mass of gapers consisted of reasonable
beings. We knew that it did, and knowing this
were aghast at the delay; at almost any instant it
might cease to be a mob and split up into reasonable beings.

"Soon, this party will break up," Moundos said.
"It is too cold for them to stay longer; besides, it
will be dinner-time."

Indeed, some of the citizens nearest to us, the
men at the extreme back of the vast crowd, who
could not see well, nor hear a word of what was
said, began to drift away, in ones and twos. Some
of them looked at us as they passed, though not
with any attention; certainly with no misgivings.
One of the Count's orderlies clambered up to us,
with the word: "Get ready; and watch for smoke
behind the Imperial Box."

We passed the word, so that our men put down their spears, and drew their light strong swords. Moundos said: "We'd better get nearer the arena. Get forward, boys." He gave a signal to the mess-captains who were watching for it; we clambered down towards the stadium. We came to a passage-way, which led through a stone vault right on to the Course.

"What's this place?" Moundos asked.

"It's the Gate of Death, Sir," I answered. "The horses and drivers who are killed in the Races—and there are always some killed, or it isn't con-sidered a Meeting—are always carried out here." Indeed, there was a big stone slab with a cross above it, where the bodies were laid.

"Just right for our stretcher-parties," Moundos said. He led the way for us through this Gate of Death on to the Course.

We crossed to the central barrier, and swung ourselves up alongside one of the big bronze wom-en who hold the banner-poles on Cup Days. From that point, we could see our men forming up, and the enormous crowd. The bands had begun to play a popular Dinner-Green song; and those thousands of men began to sing to it, all out of time, it seemed, as mass-singing so often seems, if the mass be beyond a certain size. A cloud of light smoke lifted suddenly over the roof of the Impe-rial Box: it seemed to run along the back of the buildings there, and to spread swiftly, under the draught of the wind. I could see the heads of the mob lift to watch this smoke; and, a second later, I cried: "There's The Count. He's engaged. He's at them."

At the same instant, a cry rose up from the mob rather to the left of our front; it was not a human cry; it was the sort of wail or sob that a herd of beasts might utter when between the devil and the deep sea. The bands had stopped and the song died away into this, while above it, the Barbarians raised their war-yell. The Count was plainly to be seen, with his gold helm, and the bright helms of his men, driving into the pack and forcing it towards us, or rather towards our side.

"That is what we've waited for," Moundos cried, swinging himself down into the Course. "Come on, boys; we can end this now. Shout, boys; come at them." I remember that as the three companies raised their war-yell, many of the mob turned their heads to look at us; then, instantly turned away and shrank further in towards the Imperial Box, and thrust towards it, and drove the vast assembly that way. Those nearest to the Imperial Box saw that there was no escape that way, for the barriers checked them, and the Box was on fire at the back and smoke was blinding down into the Course from it. I know, that as we ran at the mob, shouting and hooting, bright fire ran along the back of the great building so that the multitude knew itself to be trapped between a fire and the sword.

It was the most frightful thing which ever happened in our City, in any City; an earthquake would have been less fatal; a pestilence less sudden. It was said that thirty thousand men died in that awful hour. Some have said, that the Barbarians and Moundos's men were ruthless to an unarmed mob; that is not true. I had the task of helping to clear the Course in the following days; and I am certain, that few of the dead had been killed by the sword. Many died of suffocation, the smoke for a short time was very thick; but the mad jam and pressure of the multitude upon itself was the main cause of death; panic, shock, terror and the frantic struggle of unconscious man with madman killed that multitude. It was said, and I believe it, that the only few who escaped were some from the extreme right side, who got out by walking on the heads of the jammed and dead men beneath them. I saw two escape thus, with my own eyes; and no doubt many others may have had that luck.

I think that most of that crowd died swiftly and painlessly. They choked and lost consciousness and ceased. They had, perhaps, one moment of appalling terror and horror; but even this was not a human thing, suffered by individuals, it was a herd

thing, a "panic" thing, common to them all. It is
my own feeling, that these "panic" moods are of
enormous, frightful strength, and afflict each individual with the power of many thousands of
united souls, and that men are killed by the
strength of that feeling; the individual cannot
bear it. It may be that in a mood of such appalling
stress the nature of the blood is changed suddenly,
so that the heart stops.

The rebellion was broken finally in all its
branches and roots in that most terrible hour.

The nephews of Justinian went directly to the
throne, and seized Hypatius where he sat, cowed,
waiting for death. I suppose that no man has been
so madly acclaimed and so crushingly broken
within so short a time. The young naval officers
dragged him and his brother out of it, and sent
them in under guard to the Emperor. They were
put to death later. After this hour of death The
Count's men cleared Fourth Ward; Moundos's
men ended all disorder in Sixth Ward. The rebellion was broken utterly by dark that evening;
all The City was in mourning and subjection. Pa-
trols went through the streets that night, but no
one was about; all were mourning their dead and
fearing for the vengeance of the morrow.

I went out at dawn upon the morrow, in that
part where the riot had done most hurt. The City

was all burnt out on that side; it was nothing but blackened shells, and fallen roofs, with dead bodies here and there, some of looters, some of the rebels; and a defilement everywhere of The City and the idea of man. The great Church was gone, that had been The City's offering to God; the Market had gone, that was the centre of the life of The City; the Senate House was gone, that had been the centre of government; much wealth had been destroyed and much misery put into the heart; it would have been hard to find a home within the walls which did not mourn for someone or something. At a point in the ruined Market I saw the morning spreading into the eastern heaven and lighting up all the marvellous scene. Some ships coming in from the eastern waters were bringing the advanced guards of the Army, though no enemy remained for it to quell. Though the scenes which I looked upon were sad enough, and though nothing could bring back the beauty burned nor the lives spilled, there was hope in what I saw. A new day was beginning; young men were coming home to give to the new day an energy long lacking to us, and a hope to which we had been blind in the past. We had to bury the dead and begin anew.

Many years later, when The City had become the Glory of all Time, the one City to compare with Athens for her gift to the Human Imagination, I had the task of sorting the private papers of our beloved Empress, the Sovereign Lady, Theodora, after her Death.

Among these, I came upon a little case of sheets of parchment written upon in the two hands of Theodora and Justinian. Sometimes Theodora had written a suggestion, and Justinian had commented upon it; sometimes, it was the other way about. Both wrote beautiful hands; those exquisite spirits had every adornment.

The sheets must have been written by them in the frightful days of the rebellion, and in those days of almost despair which followed them, when everything had to be remade. There were seven of these sheets. It was clear from them that Theodora looked upon The City as a theatre ruined, with all the gear of dancers and musicians destroyed and the company scattered; Justinian thought of it as something that had been and might again be a City of the Holy Wisdom. In all her notes, Theodora urged that the rebuilt City should be as an amazing Theatre set for a performance of wonder, with all the citizens the performers, each perfect in his part; in his, Justinian imaged forth his concept, of the Centre of the World, about a Place of the Holy Wisdom, a Church under a Star, to which all the Wise Men of the World would turn, seeking and bringing wisdom. From these notes of theirs, those two rebuilt The City, so that each mind has left its stamp of splendour. The citizens did not want the splendour, God knows; but those two were like the Moon and the Sun, light shone from them and made all bright about them.